Perry la[y] with ma[ny] [of her] pages scattered in front of him

Her manuscript, Kristin realized nervously. "Perry?"

Looking up, he focused on her, then set aside the page in his hand. He swung his legs over the side of the bed and stood. Feeling awkward, she tightened the sash on her robe as he moved toward her. "I'm afraid I got carried away with my notes. I'm sorry..."

Before she could finish the sentence, his mouth was on hers. By the time Perry finally drew back for air, Kristin was clinging to him helplessly, her knees almost too weak to support her. "What—?"

"I love your book," he murmured against her lips. "Especially the hero."

He was grinning like a fool—which she found as endearing as it was baffling. "I'm about ten pages from finishing it. I still don't know who the blackmailer is. Why don't you put me out of my misery and tell me."

She grinned at him impishly. "You'll just have to read it for yourself."

He nuzzled her temple. "C'mon, Kristin. Tell me who it is." When she didn't respond, his hands undid the sash on her robe. Then, pushing the material off one shoulder, he said wickedly, "I have ways of making you talk...."

Dear Reader,

In 1999 Harlequin will celebrate its 50th anniversary in North America. Canadian publishing executive Richard Bonnycastle founded the company in 1949. Back then, they published a wide variety of American and British paperbacks—from mysteries and Westerns, to classics and cookbooks. In later years, the company focused on romance exclusively, and today Harlequin is the world's leading publisher of series romance fiction. Our books are sold in over one hundred countries and published in more than twenty-three languages. Love stories are a universal experience!

Harlequin Temptation is delighted to help celebrate this very special anniversary. We're throwing a bachelor auction...and you're invited! Join five of our leading authors as they put a sexy hero on the auction block. Sparks fly when the heroines get a chance to bid on their fantasy men.

In *It Takes a Hero*, bestselling author Gina Wilkins deals with a subject she knows very well—romance. What is romance novelist Kristin Cole going to do when she runs into a chronic case of writer's block? What else? She buys a hero! Gina, the author of more than fifty books, has been with Temptation since 1987 and has become a favorite with readers all over the world. Watch for Gina's By Request collection, *Holding Out For a Hero*, available in June 1999.

Each month, we strive to bring you the very best stories and writers. And we plan to keep doing that for the next fifty years!

Happy Anniversary,

Birgit Davis-Todd
Senior Editor
Harlequin Temptation

Gina Wilkins
IT TAKES A HERO

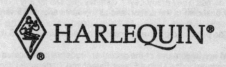

TORONTO • NEW YORK • LONDON
AMSTERDAM • PARIS • SYDNEY • HAMBURG
STOCKHOLM • ATHENS • TOKYO • MILAN • MADRID
PRAGUE • WARSAW • BUDAPEST • AUCKLAND

ISBN 0-373-25829-1

IT TAKES A HERO

Copyright © 1999 by Gina Wilkins.

Look us up on-line at: http://www.romance.net

Printed in U.S.A.

Prologue

PERRY GOODMAN STOOD backstage at the glamorous, luxurious Waldorf-Astoria and wished he were somewhere else. Anywhere else. He tugged at the collar of his tuxedo, feeling as if it were strangling him. In his work as a political strategist, he wore tuxedos often, and even liked dressing up on occasion. But tonight, he would much rather have been wearing his old, shabby Denver Broncos sweatshirt and a pair of jeans.

He usually enjoyed working a crowded room, being the center of attention, making himself and his political candidates and causes well known. That was why he'd chosen a career in behind-the-scenes politics; because he enjoyed interacting with people, because he cared deeply about his political party's agenda and wanted to make a positive difference. But on this particular evening, he'd rather be parked on his couch in front of the TV. Alone.

He peeked around the edge of the curtain at the poor schlemiel standing at the end of a runway that reminded him uncomfortably of fashion shows and beauty pageants. The glittering ballroom was filled to capacity with people—mostly women—and all eyes were turned to the latest offering in the charity bachelor auction being sponsored by Heart Books. The last Perry had heard, the bidding was up to nearly five thousand dollars for the guy.

At two hundred and fifty dollars per head for admission, in addition to the bids rolling in during the auction, the literacy groups for which the money was being raised should benefit quite nicely from the evening. That satisfying knowledge gave Perry the fortitude to lift his chin and vow to himself that he would get through this, and he would do it with style. He wouldn't have chosen on his own to stroll down that runway and offer himself for a weekend to the highest bidder, but it was all for a very good cause. Hadn't he just reminded himself that he wanted to make a positive difference—in any way he could?

And, besides, the damned Broncos had lost a game on which Perry had placed a friendly bet with an old friend of his who happened to work in Heart Books' publicity department. Perry had never welshed on a bet in his life.

He told himself he might even find the weekend—and his purchaser—amusing, which would be a nice change from some of the evenings-from-hell he'd spent since his engagement fell apart a year ago. Of course, given that the woman would probably be an avid romance novel fan, he hoped she wasn't expecting more fantasy than reality.

He'd never actually read a romance novel, and had never been particularly interested in doing so, considering them something only women would enjoy. But Perry knew when to keep his opinions to himself. For the sake of the charity, the bet he'd made, and for his own up-and-coming reputation, he would pretend interest in the books and their fans—one fan, in particular. The one who would "buy" him for a weekend.

1

MAYBE IT WAS THE CHAMPAGNE that made Kristin Cole offer several thousand dollars for a weekend with an attractive stranger. She didn't usually indulge in more than a few sips, but her vivacious table companions kept filling her glass and making witty toasts to the various bachelors who appeared on the stage at the front of the huge, crowded, glittering ballroom. Kristin found herself laughing and joining in, to the delighted approval of her mother, Sophie, who sat beside her, urging her on.

Kristin certainly hadn't intended to bid on anyone when she'd arrived at the bachelor auction. She was here because, as the author of a dozen romance novels, she wanted to support her publisher in raising money for literacy, a cause Kristin wholeheartedly supported. And because it had sounded like fun to spend an evening with her editor and some of her writer friends—as well as her mother, who'd heard about the event and had immediately decided to attend.

Kristin was also aware that this function made a convenient excuse to avoid her computer for a few days. She grimaced at the thought of that blank computer monitor waiting for her at home. Lately she'd fancied that the empty screen mirrored her painfully idea-deprived mind. And, as the deadline for her next contracted project grew closer and closer, her desperation increased.

"What's the matter, Kristin?" Sophie Cole challenged her daughter, misreading the frown. "You don't care for gorgeous stock analysts?"

Forcing her thoughts away from the problem that had been tormenting her for the past few months, Kristin glanced at the stage, then pasted on a smile and shook her head. "He's attractive enough, but I really prefer dark-haired men."

Sophie made a face. "Honey, the last thing anyone would notice about that hunk is the color of his hair. Look at those shoulders. And that nice, firm..."

"Mother." Kristin rolled her eyes as the other four women at their table laughed. "Try not to completely embarrass me, will you?"

Sophie only grinned and sipped her champagne, her eyes focused appreciatively on the latest bachelor. Sophie Cole was fifty-four, but could have passed for nearly ten years younger. Her bright red hair was artfully tousled, and she kept her figure firm and trim through exercise and constant activity. Because of her longtime, almost religious adherence to sunscreen and moisturizers, there were only a few lines around her eyes and mouth, and those had been carved by her quick, contagious smiles. Widowed for nearly twenty years, she was amusing, fun-loving, impulsive and unpredictable. And Kristin adored her, despite their differences.

To Kristin's exasperation and their dining companions' amusement, Sophie had offered to "buy a man" for her daughter's upcoming thirtieth birthday. Kristin had only glared at her and told her to forget it. After her last romantic debacle, Kristin hadn't been particularly interested in dating *any-one*, especially a total stranger.

The blond stock analyst was purchased by an ex-cited-looking woman at the table next to them. Everyone cheered as the woman—a writer Kristin had met on several occasions—triumphantly pumped the air with her fist.

"Isn't this fun?" Kristin's editor, Joyce Milhollen, asked from her seat at Kristin's left. Happily married, Joyce wasn't placing any bids, but she seemed to be enjoying the evening immensely. "I can't believe how much money is being spent to-night. The funα-raiser is going to be a huge suc-cess."

Kristin smiled and nodded. "It certainly looks like it."

"Your mother seems to be having a good time."

Kristin glanced to her right, noting that Sophie was engaged in a lively conversation with another writer and a woman who worked in the marketing department. "My mother always has a good time."

"And what about you? Are *you* enjoying the eve-ning?" Joyce studied Kristin's face as she asked the question, making Kristin wonder if Joyce had any idea of the stress she was dealing with.

Kristin answered with a breeziness she hoped was convincing. "Oh, I'm having a great time."

Someone else claimed Joyce's attention then, and Kristin almost sighed in relief. She hadn't dis-cussed her recent writing difficulties with any-one—not her editor, her agent, her friends, or even her mother. She'd been afraid that if she voiced the problem—actually said the dreaded words *writer's block*—she would only make it all the more real.

"Would you look at this one?" Sophie sighed when another bachelor was introduced. Large closed-circuit TV screens showed close-ups of the man to those who sat too far away from the stage to see him clearly.

Kristin glanced at one of those screens, noting that he looked to be in his late forties, with tanned skin, clear blue eyes and hair that had gone silver around his ruggedly handsome face. The MC, whose sparkling commentary had kept the audience laughing throughout the evening, introduced him as Jack Burnett, airline pilot. He was an avid sky diver, and his date package involved both parachutes and ballroom dancing.

"Now, there's a romance hero—and a great date," Joyce said with an appreciative sigh. "If I were you, Kristin, I'd bid on that one."

Kristin was just about to remind her editor that she didn't intend to bid on *anyone* when her mother spoke, instead.

"Sorry, darling. This one is mine." Sophie threw her hand in the air for an opening bid of a thousand dollars. Her large, splashy rings glittered in the light, easily catching the attention of the auctioneer. "Is he scrumptious or what?"

"Mother!" Kristin could almost feel her jaw dropping. "What are you *doing?*"

A woman at the front of the room raised the bid to fifteen hundred dollars. Sophie promptly bid two thousand, then answered her daughter's question. "What does it look like I'm doing? I'm buying a date with that delicious-looking man."

"A date that includes jumping out of an airplane? Have you lost your mind?"

"It's something I've always meant to try." Sophie upped her bid again against the woman at the front table.

The bidding was spirited and good-natured. And in the end, to their companions' delight and Kristin's dismay, Sophie was the winner, paying five thousand dollars for a chance to leap out of a plane with a silver-haired bachelor.

"I cannot believe you did that," Kristin muttered, making herself heard over the excited chattering around them.

"Oh, lighten up, Kristin. Wouldn't hurt you to do the same thing." Sophie refilled her daughter's champagne flute and then her own. "Let's toast my success, shall we?"

Two bachelors and several toasts later, Kristin finally stopped trying to retain her common sense. Bidding was fast and furious for the remaining bachelors, and she found herself cheering the participants as enthusiastically as the rest of the crowd. It was fun, it was all for a wonderful cause, it was a much-needed change of pace from her usual routines...why not make the most of the evening? And maybe, she told herself with a slight edge of desperation, she would go home with a brilliant idea for her book.

Maybe it was the champagne...

"And now, ladies, may I introduce Perry Goodman," the MC sang out after an introductory buildup Kristin hadn't paid much attention to. Something about politics, she thought. And a date package that included attendance at one of the big-

gest, most exclusive political fund-raiser galas of
the season, to be held later in the week, on Thursday evening.

The noisy applause that welcomed the newest
bachelor onto the stage surprised Kristin. Maybe
he wasn't a politician. Maybe he was an actor or
well-known athlete who simply planned to attend
the political gala with his date. She had rarely
heard this type of starstruck applause for a politician. She wished she'd listened a little more carefully. Leaning closer to Joyce, she asked, "Who is
this guy?"

Joyce seemed startled by the question. "You've
never heard of Perry Goodman?"

Kristin frowned in concentration. The name
sounded a little familiar...but she couldn't quite
place it. "I don't think so."

"I take it you don't follow politics?"

Wrinkling her nose, Kristin shook her head.
"Politics bores me," she admitted. "It all seems so
phony and pretentious."

"Surely you've heard of Perry Goodman, Kristin," her mother said. "He's on television all the
time. Why, he was on *Meet the Press* just last Sun-
day."

"I was probably watching the classic movie
channel, if anything," Kristin replied with a shrug.
"You know I don't follow politics, Mother. Is this
guy running for something?"

"He doesn't run, himself. He's a political strategist. He's the brains behind the campaigns of the
politicians who hire him."

"Oh." Kristin shifted her chair to give her a better view of the man who was the center of all this attention. She felt her eyes widen. "Oh, my."

Sophie laughed along with the others in response to Kristin's dumbstruck expression. "Well, this is encouraging. My daughter isn't totally immune to a stunningly good-looking young man, after all."

Stunned was exactly the word to describe Kristin's reaction as she stared at the enlarged, projected close-up of Perry Goodman. But *good-looking* was a woefully inadequate description of the man. He was...beautiful, she decided, feeling her cheeks go warm. Thick, wavy dark hair, obviously styled by an expert. Glittering hazel eyes, surrounded by thick, dark lashes. Classic, clean-cut features. A sexy smile that revealed straight white teeth. And dimples. Oh, heavens, did the man have dimples!

It occurred to her suddenly that he looked *exactly* like the hero she'd described in the book she'd been trying to write for the past few months. She couldn't have described him more closely if she'd been looking at his photograph when she'd created her hero, Nick O'Donnell.

"If I weren't married, I would bid on that one myself," Joyce murmured.

"Are you sure you don't want me to buy him for your birthday, sweetie?" Sophie asked, looking as though she needed only a hint of encouragement to jump into the opening bid.

"Forget it, Mother," Kristin replied, though her tone lacked its earlier firmness.

She couldn't seem to stop staring at him. That thick hair. Those dimples. That confident, just slightly cocky air about him. Was it possible that she *had* seen the guy on television some time and unconsciously turned him into a romance hero?

The bidding started at a thousand dollars. Within a matter of moments, it had risen to more than five thousand.

"Some lucky woman is going to have a spectacular weekend," Sophie murmured with a sigh. "Maybe I should buy him for myself. Then I'd have two great dates lined up."

As if Sophie Cole ever lacked for great dates, Kristin thought wryly. Sophie's social calendar made her daughter's look positively boring. Probably because it *was* boring, she thought with a slight wince. Since her painful breakup with Jim Hooper, she hadn't met anyone she trusted enough to risk dating again. She'd assured her mother repeatedly that she wouldn't allow one terrible mistake to ruin her life forever, but it hadn't been easy to recover from an affair that had left her doubting her ability to know a good man when she saw one.

Someone offered fifty-five hundred dollars for the date with Perry Goodman. Someone else immediately upped it to six thousand. The crowd cheered and called for more. On the stage, and on the giant TV screens, Perry's smile took on a bemused edge that only made him more appealing, in Kristin's opinion.

He looked directly at the camera, his eyes glittering in the bright lighting. Staring at the screen, Kristin had the unsettling sensation that he was looking directly at her. Beckoning her. Tempting her...

She thought of all the anguish she'd been through, trying to pump some life into a story that had refused to cooperate. She'd become so frustrated with it that she'd begun to panic, wondering if she was going to have to buy back her contract or try to develop another idea in time to make her deadline. There'd been moments when she'd worried that she would never be able to write again. Even knowing other writers often struggled with the same fears hadn't comforted her.

She wondered if spending a weekend with a man who could have stepped directly from the pages of her novel would help inspire her to finish it.

She felt her hand go into the air, though she didn't remember actually making a decision to place a bid.

"All right, Kristin!" someone at the table called out. Sophie applauded fervently. Kristin kept her eyes on the screen and raised her hand again when someone outbid her by five hundred dollars.

This wasn't an entirely crazy thing to do, she assured herself, trying to rationalize her own behavior. If there was any chance that she could salvage her career by drawing inspiration from a real-life hero, she would be foolish *not* to grab the chance. Not only would she be making a deductible donation to a very worthwhile charity, she would be helping herself in the process. All in all, it made perfect sense.

"Sold for ten thousand dollars!" the MC announced a few minutes later, looking directly at Kristin.

Kristin sank bonelessly into her seat, her knees feeling suddenly too weak to support her. She wondered what on earth had gotten into her as her mother blew a jubilant kiss toward the man on the stage.

She had just paid ten *thousand* dollars for a weekend with a stranger!

She must be even more desperate about her writing than she'd realized. After all, how many writers had to buy a "hero."

KRISTIN ARRANGED TO STAY in New York during the ensuing days between the auction and the Thursday-evening-and-all-day-Friday date package she had "purchased." She met several times that week with her agent and editor, breezily—and, she hoped, convincingly—assuring them that she was making great headway on her contracted book, and had no concerns about making her deadlines. Sophie stayed in New York for two days after the auction, and she and Kristin did some shopping— Sophie urging Kristin to buy more daring and adventurous outfits for her wardrobe, Kristin quietly purchasing the same classic, conservative styles she had long preferred.

Kristin never visited New York without seeing at least two Broadway productions, and she thoroughly enjoyed both of the shows she attended during this visit. During those precious hours, she allowed herself to be entertained and transported away from her problems and into the worlds created on stage. Not once during the shows did she think of her deadlines or plotting crises or the impending gala, all of which were making her a nervous wreck.

After several days of reflection, she had come to the conclusion that she must have been temporarily insane when she started bidding on that handsome politician. The champagne, the laughter and teasing, the lights and glitter, the fact that he looked so much like the hero she'd been struggling to bring to life in her book...all those circumstances combined must have gone straight to her stress-scrambled head.

Just what had she thought she would do, follow the guy around with a notebook, jotting down every interesting thing he said? Had she thought she would somehow be transformed for a weekend into the tall, glamorous, witty pediatrician she'd created as her heroine? Hah. She couldn't even seem to be witty on paper these days.

She knew nothing and cared less about politics. She didn't particularly like snooty, pretentious affairs—and the exclusive, five-thousand-dollar-a-ticket, political fund-raiser ball Perry Goodman was taking her to would surely be both. It wouldn't even benefit the party she usually voted for.

How was this going to help her finish her book? As it was, she'd only managed to put off working on it for another week. She'd tried to write in her hotel room with her portable computer, but had found herself staring yet again at an impatiently blinking cursor, while her mind remained stubbornly blank. Each time, she'd finally turned off the computer and escaped the room in search of distraction—any distraction.

And maybe that's what this whole date was, she decided as she dressed for the gala. She turned to the mirror for one final check of her appearance. Maybe it was just another attempt to distract herself, to put off confronting her writing problems.

She'd heard other writers talk about furiously cleaning closets or organizing pantries or alphabetizing the contents of their refrigerators—anything to avoid facing their worst fears. Was she doing the same thing under the guise of "researching" her hero?

She studied her reflection somberly, noting that her floor-length, sleeveless black sheath and strappy high heels made her look a bit taller than her five feet three inches, and that the cut of the dress minimized the six or seven pounds she'd gained from stress-induced eating during the past few months. She had done her best to fit in with the sleek, sophisticated, elegant crowd with whom she would be mingling for the evening, yet she was well aware that the image was mostly illusion.

But she made her living creating illusion, she reminded herself. She could handle one evening of fantasy.

Kristin and Perry had arranged by telephone to meet at the hotel where the gala was being held—her choice—rather than having him pick her up. He'd promised to send a limo, and a glance at her watch told her it was time to head down for the lobby.

At the last minute, she slipped a small notebook into her bag before leaving her room. Just in case…

PERRY HADN'T HAD A CHANCE to meet the woman who'd "bought" him at the bachelor auction. There'd been several bachelors auctioned after him, and Perry had had to leave before the event ended to catch a flight home to D.C.

Because of the bright lights that had been trained

on him during the auction, and the large number of people seated in the ballroom, Perry had had difficulty making out individual faces. He'd smiled in the general direction of the women who'd placed bids, but their features had been blurred. The final bid had come from somewhere in the middle of the room. The only woman Perry had seen clearly at that table had stood out because of her bright red hair and the masses of sparkling jewelry she'd worn with her deep purple dress. She'd blown a kiss at him when he'd turned to leave the stage.

When he'd been told later that his date package had been purchased by a multipublished, bestselling romance writer named Kristin Cole, he'd concluded that the red-haired woman must be the one, and he'd congratulated himself on his powers of deduction. With her conspicuous appearance and extroverted manner, the woman met his preconceived notion of how a successful romance writer might look. She obviously was much older than Perry's thirty-six years, but she'd had a contagious smile that made him suspect she would be an amusing companion. He looked forward to meeting her.

A festive, glittering evening lay ahead for them. Perry generally enjoyed these events, even though attending them was part of his job. He was working when he mingled with the other guests—but then, Perry was always working. A few people—notably his ex-fiancée—had accused him of being more than a bit compulsive about his job. And about a few other things, as well, he admitted ruefully.

He huddled with a couple of his associates as he

waited for his date to arrive. He was dressed in evening clothes again, as were his companions, but they might as well have been wearing business suits. They were on the job, and they took their work very seriously. Even Perry's choice to bring his bachelor-auction date to this event had been thoughtfully calculated; it enhanced his own reputation to be seen as a man who would commit himself so personally to advancing literacy, and it gave him a chance to point out that his political party had always been firmly committed to advances in education.

"Make sure," Perry told one of his aides, "that Senator Henley greets everyone in the room, and that he's photographed with the specific individuals we mentioned earlier."

Elspeth Moore nodded briskly. "I'll keep him on track."

"Good. Marcus…" Perry turned to the man standing at Elspeth's side.

"Yes, Perry?"

"Keep an eye on Mrs. Henley, will you? Try to stay between her and Senator O'Malley's wife, as much as possible. And between Mrs. Henley and the champagne, if you can."

Marcus's coffee-colored face lit with a wry smile. "I'll try."

"Elspeth, you'll be available to assist Congressman Nalley, if he needs you, in addition to helping Senator Henley?"

"Of course, Perry. Um, weren't you bringing a date this evening?"

His staff's teasing smiles caused Perry to grin wryly. "As you are both well aware, I will have someone joining me this evening as part of my contribution to Heart Books' fund-raiser for literacy last weekend. She's a bestselling romance novelist, and I'm sure she'll be a very interesting companion for the evening. I hope you'll make an effort to welcome her."

"I heard she paid ten thousand dollars to spend an evening with you," Marcus quipped. "Wonder how long it'll take her to figure out she got gypped?"

"If all she wanted was to attend this event, she could have saved five thousand and simply bought a ticket," Elspeth agreed impishly. "She wouldn't have had to spend the whole evening with Perry that way."

"Yeah, but tickets to this thing have been sold out for months," Marcus reminded her. "Maybe coming with Perry was the only way she could get in."

"Is it so hard to believe that she might have *wanted* to spend an evening in my company?"

Marcus and Elspeth both grinned at Perry and said in unison, "Yes."

"Thanks a lot, you guys. With friends like you..."

"So, Perry, you think she'll want you to pose for the cover of one of her books? Maybe you could take off your shirt and pretend you have biceps to flex."

"Okay, Marcus, that's enough."

"He'd like that," Elspeth taunted. "A chance to get his pretty face in another medium."

"Are you two quite finished?"

"He's always rather fancied himself as the hero

type," Marcus murmured, not notably intimidated by Perry's exasperation. "Boldly braving the opposing party to advance his candidates, carrying the banner of his beliefs and ideals."

Perry glanced pointedly at his watch. "The gala is about to start. Don't you both have things to do?"

"Oh, c'mon, Perry. We want to meet the woman who thought you were worth ten thousand bucks."

Perry frowned at Marcus. "Would you—"

"Mr. Goodman?"

Hearing his name, Perry gave his aides a warning glance, then turned to meet his date.

So much for his powers of deduction, he thought. If this was Kristin Cole, she couldn't have been more different from the red-haired woman he'd assumed he'd be spending the weekend with.

The woman standing in front of him now was no more than thirty years old—at the most—and had subdued brown hair worn in a neat, conservative upsweep. Her figure-hugging black dress revealed very nice curves, and her jewelry was understated and elegant. Her features were pleasant—more pretty than beautiful—but her brown eyes were guarded as she studied him with an assessing manner that made him fancy she was preparing to describe him later to a police artist.

She looked, he thought, exactly like the type of woman he could take home to his mother. Like a woman who would easily earn his demanding family's approval.

Maybe this wasn't Kristin Cole. Maybe this was someone who'd recognized him and wanted to talk politics. "I'm Perry Goodman," he confirmed, just a hint of question in his voice.

She held out her hand. "I'm Kristin Cole. Your, um, date for the evening."

He made sure his surprise didn't show in the smile he flashed her as he took her hand. "I've been looking forward to meeting you. I've heard some great things about your writing. One of my co-workers has been singing your praises all week. I only wish I'd had a chance to read one of your books, which I'll certainly do as soon as I find time."

He turned then to his visibly curious aides. "Kristin Cole, these are my associates, Elspeth Moore and Marcus Williams."

"Nice to meet you, Ms. Cole," Marcus said as Elspeth murmured a polite greeting. "We understand you made a very generous donation to literacy last weekend."

Kristin smiled a little. "My publisher has always been a supporter of literacy programs, as well as many other worthwhile charities. I try to participate whenever I get the chance."

"Perry told us you've written twelve books," Elspeth said with an easy smile. "Where do you get all your ideas, Ms. Cole?"

"Please, call me Kristin. And ideas are the fun part of my job. I find them in many places."

Perry glanced again at his watch, deciding he'd better rescue his date before Elspeth and Marcus started teasing her as they had been doing to him.

"We'd better head for the ballroom," he said, thinking he didn't want Mrs. Henley to get a head start on the champagne—or on Senator O'Malley's wife. The two women were lifelong rivals whose husbands were both considering a run for the presidency, and despite their usual political savvy, fireworks had erupted the last time they'd attended an event together.

Perry was ironically aware that the public would tolerate heated words between the two candidates, but their wives were expected to smile and be gracious, whatever the circumstances. And it was Perry's job to give the public exactly what it wanted.

Once his aides had departed, Perry turned back to Kristin, finding her watching him again with that thoughtful, appraising manner that made him uncharacteristically self-conscious. Falling back, as he often did, on the innate charm that had served him so well for so long, he gave her his most winning smile and extended his arm to her. "Shall we join the party?"

The smile she gave in return was sweet enough to make him suddenly swallow. "Yes, let's," she murmured, and slid her hand beneath his arm.

This evening might just prove to be very interesting, after all, Perry thought, breathing in her light floral scent and becoming very aware of the feminine sway of her hips as she walked sedately at his side. Kristin Cole wasn't at all what he'd expected, but she was most definitely intriguing.

2

KRISTIN WAS STARSTRUCK, and it was all she could do not to let it show. It would have been difficult *not* to be starstruck during the hours that followed her meeting with Perry Goodman in the lobby of the exclusive Manhattan hotel in which the gala was being held. Most of the guests had come in through a separate entrance, and were already mingling in the ballroom when Kristin walked in at Perry's side.

On the stage, the first of several prominent entertainers was singing a song that had made him famous, backed up by an excellent orchestra. Among the faces in the crowd were some that Kristin had seen in movies or in television, others she'd read about in society magazines, and still others who were seen most often on the floors of the House and Senate.

"Hey, Perry, how's it going?" a striking young man asked as he passed them without pausing.

"Going great, thanks," Perry replied genially, though the man hadn't lingered for an answer.

Kristin craned her head around, trying not to be too obvious about it. "Was that…?"

Perry's mouth quirked upward. "Yes. Did you catch his last action film?"

"No. It looked a bit violent for my taste."

"You like happily-ever-after endings?"

"When I can get them," Kristin agreed. She glanced up a bit shyly at the even more handsome and fascinating man—in her own humble opinion—at her side. "What about you, Mr. Goodman? What type of films do you enjoy?"

"It's Perry," he said with a chuckle. "And I don't get to see many films. I tend to be too busy dealing with reality."

"And I suppose you only read newsmagazines and opinion polls?"

"And the occasional tell-all Washington nonfiction blockbuster," he agreed. "Just in case someone quotes me incorrectly."

She studied him gravely, wondering if being quoted correctly was all he worried about. She hadn't met many political insiders, and the opinions she'd formed about them from what she'd read and heard had not been particularly positive. So far, Perry Goodman, for all his pretty smiles and sexy dimples, hadn't done much to change her mind.

Oh, he was certainly charming. Unfailingly polite. He said all the right things, made all the right moves. It was almost as if he practiced being perfect. Maybe he did…wasn't that all part of his job?

Kristin had fallen a few times before for men with pretty faces, and she'd concluded that it took a lot more to impress her. She had also learned— the hard way—that appearances could be painfully deceiving. Some men were very good at saying all the right things with such apparent sincerity that few people doubted them. But they didn't mean a word of it. Jim Hooper had impressed her with a handsome face and attentive manner, yet she had learned, to her sorrow, that there wasn't anything behind it. She intended to be much more careful when it came to smooth-talking men.

Which didn't mean, she thought as Perry flashed her yet another wickedly boyish grin, that she couldn't enjoy spending one fantasy evening with this one.

And fantasy it was. For the next few hours, Kristin mingled with the rich and famous, as though this was something she did all the time. Perry introduced her to actors and singers and socialites and business giants. She spent several fascinating minutes chatting with a woman senator she'd always admired. She "talked shop" with a *New York Times* bestselling mystery writer she hadn't had the opportunity to meet before.

Perry made no secret of the circumstances that had put them together for the evening; in fact, he seemed to relish telling everyone that Kristin had "bought" him with a generous contribution to charity. She cynically suspected that he considered his own participation politically advantageous. He even arranged to have them photographed by several of the society-page photographers in attendance, making sure Senator Henley—whose reelection campaign Perry was spearheading—was included in a couple of the shots.

Kristin was on her best behavior all evening. She sipped champagne and nibbled hors d'oeuvres and paid close attention to what others were saying. She didn't drift off into daydreaming, as she had tended to do since childhood whenever she was bored or distracted. She kept her few political opinions to herself when they conflicted with those expressed by others around her—Perry, included. She wasn't here for political reasons, she reminded herself, but for charitable ones. She was a writer, an entertainer, not a policy maker.

Though this was hardly her usual milieu, Kristin wasn't really nervous during the evening. Maybe Perry's continuous presence at her side helped. He was so completely at ease that she couldn't help but relax. Though there were times when she sensed his attention was focused elsewhere—usually on his candidates—she didn't mind. After all, she was busily making mental notes of everything she might be able to use in a book.

A beautiful woman with dark auburn hair and truly amazing breasts spilling out the top of a gorgeous black dress approached them with a faint smile for Perry and a curious look at Kristin. "Hello, Perry. It's been a while."

Kristin noted that his smile looked a bit strained, for the first time all evening. "Hi, Jennifer. How've you been?"

"Fine, thank you. And you?"

"Great. I heard you just got back from Europe."

"Italy," she confirmed. "It was lovely."

This was the most stilted conversation Kristin had heard all evening. It was quite obvious that Perry and Jennifer had a personal history. They must have made a beautiful couple, she thought, studying them discreetly, but she'd guess from their behavior now that it had ended unpleasantly.

Jennifer turned to Kristin. "I'm sorry, we're being rude. Since Perry has neglected to introduce us, I'm Jennifer Craig. And you are…?"

The dig at Perry was subtle, but sharp. Kristin cleared her throat. "I'm Kristin Cole."

"Elspeth mentioned that you 'bought' Perry at a charity bachelor auction."

Kristin smiled. "Yes. He very generously donated his time to the literacy fund-raiser."

Jennifer lifted a perfectly arched eyebrow. "As busy as Perry usually is, it's amazing he found time to donate to any charity, no matter how worthwhile."

Kristin heard the message embedded in the comment. Whatever had been between Jennifer and Perry, his busy schedule had been a serious problem for them.

"I'm learning to manage my time a bit better than I used to," Perry said quietly. "This fund-raiser was important. I found the time for it."

Jennifer studied him somberly for several long moments. "That's nice to hear," she said finally. "Maybe you've learned there are some things more important than the latest polls."

She turned to Kristin without giving Perry a chance to respond. "It was very nice to meet you, Kristin. I hope you enjoy the rest of the evening. Now, if you'll excuse me, my friend is waiting for me. See you, Perry."

"See you, Jenn," he replied. He watched her walk away, then turned to Kristin. "I'm thirsty," he said, smiling as brightly as he had before the encounter with Jennifer. "Want some champagne?"

She nodded and accompanied him to the nearest champagne fountain. She noticed that Perry didn't look over his shoulder as they moved away. Apparently, he wanted to forget all about the encounter with Jennifer Craig.

There was dancing later in the evening, after the guests had been welcomed by several prominent speakers. Kristin danced several times with Perry and then with the quarterback of her favorite professional football team. Perry arranged that dance for her after she spotted the athlete and mentioned how much she enjoyed following the team. Before the evening ended, she'd danced with so many celebrities that she knew her mother would be both thrilled and envious when Kristin told her about it later.

She saved the last dance for Perry. Despite all her mental precautions, she couldn't prevent a little thrill of reaction from coursing through her when he took her in his arms. This slim, graceful male had quite a nice body hidden behind his conservative evening wear, she couldn't help thinking as he pulled her close on the pretext of being able to converse while they danced. "Have you had a nice time?" he asked her.

"I've had a lovely time," she answered, determinedly pulling her attention away from his broad chest and strong thighs.

"Is there anyone you haven't met that you would like me to introduce you to?"

She laughed and shook her head. "I'll never remember everyone I've met tonight. But thank you for being such a gracious host."

"I've enjoyed it," he said, looking sincere—not that she put much stock in that, since she knew looking sincere was a successful politician's primary talent.

"Most of the guests seem to have left," she commented, glancing around the emptying ballroom.

"Yes. They've made sure their names will be included in all the society-page reports tomorrow, and now they're off to whatever forms of entertainment they really prefer."

She looked up at him, wondering how *he* really felt about splashy galas like this one—and the people who attended them. "Was the evening a success? In terms of the fund-raising goals, I mean."

"A great success—in all respects," he replied, looking satisfied.

"I didn't hear many people talking politics tonight."

He shrugged. "Tonight wasn't about politics, per se. Tonight was about money. And a great deal of it was raised. Interesting, isn't it, that you and I have spent two weekends now raising money for worthwhile causes?"

Kristin bit her lip, unable to prevent a quick frown, when he compared the bachelor auction with tonight's event. She was passionately in favor of raising money for charities such as the literacy project. She'd donated to bake sales for churches, walkathons for medical research, car washes for high school cheerleaders, rummage sales for the local humane society. She'd bought cases of Girl Scout cookies and spent hours reading to schoolchildren, encouraging them to pursue their dreams as she had pursued her dream of writing. But she was having a hard time believing that any of those causes belonged in the same category as raising money to make sure Perry's political cronies were put into office.

Perry's gaze narrowed on her face. "Is something wrong, Kristin?"

She deliberately cleared her expression. "No, of course not. I'm glad your fund-raiser was a success. You must be very pleased."

He looked as though he might question her more, but the song ended. Maybe she only imagined it, but Perry seemed reluctant to release her. He held on just for a moment after the music died away, studying Kristin's face, as if wondering what she was thinking. She fervently hoped her thoughts didn't show in her eyes, since she'd been doing her best not to let him see that she had been thoroughly dazzled by him.

As if to give her an out, Marcus Williams appeared at Perry's side. "Perry, I need to talk to you about something," he said a bit apologetically.

"What is it, Marcus? Has Mrs. Henley…?"

Kristin wondered why Perry seemed worried as he asked about the senator's wife. But Marcus shook his head. "No, she's fine. The thing is, I've just heard that you've been requested to appear on *Friday Morning Update* tomorrow. They're going to be talking about the vice president's latest gaffe. It was thought best if you go on to represent Senator Henley, rather than sending him to comment directly."

Kristin watched as Perry's expression turned instantly speculative. She could almost see him weighing pros and cons, looking for pitfalls, mentally writing sound bites. And then he nodded. "It probably is best if I do the talking this time. We don't want Robert to look too opportunistic."

Kristin managed not to roll her eyes. The political process was so calculated. Every word measured, every action debated. Who wanted to live that way?

Perry glanced suddenly at Kristin, making her hastily clear her expression. "About our plans for tomorrow..." he began.

"Don't let me keep you from your work. I quite understand if you need to cancel."

He shook his head. "I have no intention of canceling. *Friday Morning Update* is taped very early. All I need to do is set our meeting time back half an hour. I'll pick you up at ten, rather than nine-thirty, if that's all right with you."

"Yes, of course, but are you sure you have time? Tonight was certainly well worth the contribution I made to the literacy auction, anyway, and I really should get back to work, myself."

"You bought a package that included an outing tomorrow," Perry said stubbornly. "I'll pick you up at ten."

Sensing that his pride had come into play, Kristin nodded and acquiesced. "All right. I'll be ready at ten."

"Great. Marcus, you'll make the changes in arrangements for us?"

"You bet."

"Thanks." He glanced at his watch. "Since I'm getting such an early start in the morning, I'd better call it a night. Kristin, are you ready to go?"

"Yes." She smiled and wrinkled her nose. "To be honest, it's already past my usual bedtime. I tend to be one of those early-to-bed, early-to-rise types."

Perry chuckled. "I tend to be late-to-bed, early-to-rise. I've learned to get by on four or five hours' sleep most nights."

"Less, at times," Marcus agreed wryly.

After a few more instructions for his aide, Perry escorted Kristin to the waiting limousine. She glanced over her shoulder as they left the ballroom. It really had been a special evening, she thought a bit wistfully.

THE FEW PEOPLE WHO WERE in the lobby of Kristin's hotel so late on this Thursday evening glanced their way as Perry escorted her through the front doors. She knew their evening clothes made them stand out from the more casually dressed tourists and business travelers. And she could spot the ones who recognized Perry, though most of them were fairly discreet about it.

Kristin suspected Perry would have been noticed even if he wasn't a regular on television talk shows. Men would heed the confident way he walked; women would be drawn to his masculine grace and beauty. Kristin was more accustomed to blending into crowds without being noticed, having always considered herself an observer rather than a participant. Yet she admitted to herself that there was a nice ego-boost to being seen with a man like Perry Goodman, if only for one evening.

She just hoped all the mental notes she'd made during the past few hours would be of use to her when she sat down at her computer again.

Perry insisted on walking her to her room, though she assured him she could make it by herself. "What kind of date would this be if I didn't see you all the way home?" he chided good-naturedly, stepping into the elevator with her.

She knew he was trying to be polite, that he was filling the role of "perfect date" as best he could. The whole evening had been an illusion, and Kristin thought she'd fit in very well, considering that she'd spent the entire time pretending. She wondered if Perry would be quite so persistent about spending more time with her if he had seen the *real* Kristin Cole.

She couldn't help wondering if there was more to Perry Goodman than the polished, practiced politician he'd shown her during the evening.

There was no one else in her hallway when she and Perry stepped off the elevator. Her key card in her hand, she turned to him at her door. "Thank you again for a very interesting evening," she said, in a low voice.

Perry moved a step closer, his manner casual, nonthreatening, his eyes gleaming with humor. "So this is the end of the first half of our ten-thousand-dollar date."

Kristin had to chuckle at his wording, though she was suddenly, vividly aware that she and Perry were alone together for the first time. "Yes, I suppose it is."

"I'm not sure you got your money's worth," he said with a crooked, self-deprecating smile.

"I'm quite sure I did," she replied airily. Now, if only she could manage to squeeze a few chapters out of the experience…

"There's still one small detail we should take care of before we can officially call it a night."

She didn't trust his innocent expression for a moment. Her pulse was suddenly showing an odd tendency to race. "What small detail?"

"The good-night kiss. It is customary, you know, at the end of a date."

Kristin cleared her throat. "This wasn't exactly a date."

"Of course it was. The nicest date I've had in quite a while, actually."

There hadn't been any overt flirtation in Perry's manner toward her earlier. But he was most definitely flirting now. And Kristin would have had to have been made of stone not to respond. She swallowed. "That's a very nice thing to say. But…"

"One little kiss," he murmured, laying a hand against the side of her face. "Just to make it official."

She couldn't help smiling a little, though her heart was now tap-dancing nervously in her chest. Her hands rose to his shoulders, and she was vividly aware again of how solid he was. "I suppose there's no harm in one little kiss."

"No harm at all," he assured her. And then he lowered his mouth to hers.

The moment his lips touched hers, Kristin realized that this wasn't going to be a "little" kiss. This, she thought dazedly as his mouth moved against hers, was a toe-curling, mind-spinning, bell-ringing humdinger. And, oh, was she enjoying it!

When Perry finally drew back for oxygen, Kristin found herself staring up at him, unable to think of anything to say. What witty, sophisticated thing would one of her heroines say at this point? Kristin was quite sure it wouldn't be "Holy Moses!"

Perry didn't step away. Instead, he leaned close again and murmured, "Maybe just one more..."

Kristin closed her eyes and lifted her face again. Just one more...

Amazingly enough, the second kiss was as spectacular as the first. Kristin's knees wobbled; she leaned against Perry for support. His arms went around her—and she wasn't sure if he was holding her up or himself. She gasped for breath when he finally lifted his head.

"I could come in for a little while...." he said, his voice husky.

As tempted as she was to agree, Kristin managed to smile and shake her head. "We have a big day ahead of us tomorrow. I'd better get some rest."

He looked momentarily disappointed, then he smiled and stepped back. "Well, it was worth a shot. I'll see you in the morning, Kristin. Sleep well."

"Good night, Perry."

She turned and opened her door. Before she stepped inside, she couldn't resist looking over her shoulder. Perry was waiting for an elevator. Looking elegantly at ease in his tuxedo, he stood with one hand propped against the wall. His dark hair was just a bit rumpled, as if by an errant breeze— or a woman's fingers. He looked so utterly delicious that her mouth almost watered.

Before she could be tempted to drag him into the room with her, Kristin hastily went inside and closed the door. And then fastened all the locks. Only then did she allow herself to sag against the door and mutter, "Holy Moses!"

KRISTIN TURNED ON the television as she dressed the next morning, tuning in to *Friday Morning Update*—a program she never watched at home. Perry wasn't the first guest, and before fifteen minutes of the program were up, Kristin's eyes were already glazing over with boredom. Two representatives from opposing philosophies were debating an obscure issue, and Kristin had never heard so much petty bickering and sarcastic name-calling in her life.

And then Perry came on screen. Kristin could see right away why he was so popular on the talk show circuit. The camera loved him. When he talked, Kristin had the oddest sensation that he was speaking just to her, and she had no doubt other viewers felt the same way. He presented his case clearly, concisely, congenially, and when his counterpart from the other party tried to draw him into a heated argument, Perry was able to hold his own without resorting to personal attacks.

Kristin didn't have to agree with everything he said in order to admire his style. His presentation was flawless. Again, it was that very perfection that nagged at her. Just who was the real Perry Goodman? Was he no more than the glossy surface he presented to the public? Was he really deeply committed to the ideals he espoused, or would he argue as eloquently for the other side if paid enough to do so?

Did he ever lose his temper or say something stupid? Had he ever spilled a drink on a head of state or walked out of a rest room with toilet paper clinging to his shoe or even temporarily totally lost his cool?

It occurred to her that she really hadn't spent enough time with him to get to know the real Perry. She knew that if he was judging her on the time they'd been together so far, he probably had a far different mental picture of Kristin Cole than what she was really like. Everything had just happened to go right for her last night; she hadn't said or done anything foolish—except, perhaps, for those good-night kisses that had left her tingling long after she'd closed herself into her room. She blamed those on the champagne she'd sipped during the evening, which made a very convenient excuse for her uncharacteristic behavior.

She only hoped she could make it through one more day with "Perfect Perry" without doing something utterly stupid.

Nothing she saw in her reflection in the mirror gave her immediate cause for concern. She'd chosen to wear a loose ecru jacket over a matching shell and soft pleated slacks. She'd added a gold chain and small gold hoop earrings, leaving her hair loose to her shoulders. It was an outfit that was comfortable and yet sophisticated enough for almost anything Perry had planned for the day.

Pushing her sleeves up on her arms, she donned her watch and a gold bracelet, then slipped a gold-and-ruby ring on her right hand. After sliding her feet into bone pumps, she was ready. And she was seriously tempted to call Perry and cancel the whole thing. Wouldn't it be best to quit while she was ahead? she wondered, knowing her mother would be scandalized at the very idea.

Her telephone rang and she picked it up, wondering if Perry had already made it from the television studio—or if he, perhaps, had found it necessary to cancel their plans. A cowardly part of her almost hoped that was it.

But it was Sophie who spoke when Kristin answered. "Oh, good, you're still in. How's your ten-thousand-dollar date going?"

Sophie had returned to her home in Raleigh, North Carolina, but she'd been reluctant to leave New York. She had wanted to stay and meet Perry Goodman, and be on the scene to make sure Kristin took full advantage of the weekend. Kristin had been relieved that her mother's social obligations had required her to return home. "Everything is fine, Mother."

"Details, darling. I want details. I've been reading the society reports about the gala last night. Was it as fabulous as it sounds? Did you get to meet anyone famous?"

"Everyone I met was famous, I think," Kristin answered wryly. "And, yes, it was fabulous. Like something out of a glitz novel." The kind of book she had never particularly wanted to write, she couldn't help thinking.

"And what's on the agenda for today?"

"I'm not sure. The date package said only that it was to include a champagne brunch, followed by 'a day of surprises.'" And Kristin had already vowed that she was drinking no more than a sip of the champagne.

"That sounds enticing. I can't wait to hear all about it."

"I'll call you as soon as I get back home tomorrow," Kristin promised. "What about your own date? When are you planning to jump out of that plane? I'd like to know so I'll be sure and spend that entire day in church, praying to the patron saint of crazy women."

Sophie laughed. "We're going next weekend. And I am not crazy, thank you very much. I'm simply adventurous. As I've tried unsuccessfully to raise you to be."

"Hey, I'm spending a weekend with a politician, aren't I? I consider that pretty adventurous."

"I saw him on *Friday Morning Update*. The man is divine, Kristin. I certainly hope he's as charming in person as he appears on screen."

"Yes, he's quite charming." She didn't add that he could have taught classes in the trait—probably did so with his candidates, for all she knew.

"Do you like him?"

"He's very nice."

"Does he like you?"

"Mother, he doesn't even know me. We've only spent a few hours together."

"Did he kiss you?"

"Mother!"

"That means he did," Sophie concluded in satisfaction. "Was he good?"

"I am not having this conversation."

"He didn't happen to spend the night, did he?"

"*Mother!*"

"He didn't," Sophie sighed, easily interpreting her daughter's responses. "Oh, well, there's always tonight."

"I'm hanging up now."

"I'm only trying to put a little spice in your life, darling. One really can't have an on-going relationship with a computer."

"Nor do I expect to have an on-going relationship with Perry Goodman," Kristin replied tartly. "This weekend is strictly to benefit charity—on both of our parts. After today, I doubt that we'll ever see each other again."

Sophie sighed gustily. "A mother can dream, can't she?"

"I'll repeat—I had no intention of buying a boyfriend last weekend. I made a donation to my favorite charity, and this weekend is part of the package. Maybe I'll even get some material for a book out of it. But that's all. Okay?"

Sophie muttered something Kristin didn't quite understand. She did not ask her to repeat it. "I have to go now, Mother. Perry's picking me up soon. I'll call you when I get home tomorrow."

She hung up before her mother could harass her further. And then she pushed a hand through her hair and grimaced, wondering what Perry had thought of her after she'd responded so fervently to his kisses. She certainly hoped he didn't consider her some sort of a political groupie or a desperate single woman who'd tried to buy a romance.

Maybe last night she'd been Cinderella at the ball. But Perry would find her very different today. She was as serious about her job as he was about his. She put her notebook in her purse, along with one of the lightweight disposable cameras she favored on research outings.

This wasn't a date, she told herself firmly. The whole purpose of this weekend—other than the charity donation, of course—was to help her with her book. She would not forget that today. Which meant no more kisses, she told herself, tossing her head in renewed determination. No matter how tempting they might be.

Her telephone rang again. Hoping it wasn't her mother, she answered warily.

"Ms. Cole? Mr. Goodman is waiting for you in the lobby," a rather mechanical voice informed her.

"Thank you. I'll be right down."

She hung up the phone and drew a deep breath, then tucked her purse beneath her arm and headed for the door.

3

THE WAY HER PULSE fluttered when Kristin saw Perry waiting in the lobby let her know she hadn't been entirely successful in convincing herself that today was "strictly business." He looked every bit as delicious in a Polo shirt and neatly pressed khakis as he looked in formal evening clothes. And when he gave her a warm smile of greeting, her mind was flooded with memories of the kisses they had shared only hours before.

In reaction to her unwelcome physical responses, her voice was even cooler than she'd intended. "Good morning, Perry."

His left eyebrow rose just a fraction, but his own greeting was much friendlier. "Good morning, Kristin. You look lovely."

"Thank you." She could think of nothing to add.

"Ready for your 'day of surprises'?" he asked with a chuckle, quoting the bachelor auction brochure.

"Yes," she lied. "What will we be doing?"

He shook a finger at her. "If I tell you now, it won't be a surprise."

She hoped her smile didn't look as forced as it felt. She was ready to have this day behind her, to stop playing at being charming with Perry Goodman and get back to her work. At least, she hoped she would be able to work now. She didn't want to face the possibility that she would return to her computer only to discover that her creativity was still on an extended vacation.

Perry escorted her out of the hotel to a limousine. "Champagne?" he asked, once they were settled inside the car.

Still blaming the beverage for her recent uncharacteristic behavior, Kristin shook her head. "No, thank you."

"We have fruit juice, sodas or sparkling water," he offered instead, peering into the tiny refrigerator.

"I'm fine, thank you. I had coffee and juice in my room."

Perry settled back in his seat. "We didn't have a chance to talk much last night. Tell me about yourself, Kristin."

He sounded like one of the talk show hosts he spent so much time with. "What do you want to know?"

Undeterred by her reserved manner, he forged on. "You've written a dozen books, I understand. How long have you been writing?"

"I've been published for five years," she replied, not bothering to add that she'd been penning stories almost since the day she'd first learned to hold a pencil. Telling stories had always been such a joy for her. So easy—until about two months ago.

"What made you choose to write romance novels?"

"I write what I enjoy reading. Romance addresses issues that appeal to me—love, friendship, loyalty, family connections, children. Within the framework of a love story, I have the freedom to write comedy, drama, adventure, fantasy... anything I want. I find it both satisfying and challenging."

More challenging than satisfying at the moment, but she was hoping to correct that.

"Do you think you'll ever write a real book?"

She raised both eyebrows. It wasn't the first time she'd been asked that insensitive question, but she hadn't expected it from Perry. "I've written twelve 'real' books."

He had the grace to flush. "I didn't mean that the way it sounded. I, er, meant to ask if you had any plans to write something other than a romance."

"Not at this point. It just depends on where my muse takes me in the future."

He cleared his throat, still looking a bit disconcerted. Kristin found herself almost relieved that he could say something awkward occasionally, even if it was at her expense. His faux pas made him seem a bit less perfect.

He deliberately changed the subject. "You said last night you live in Raleigh, North Carolina?"

"Not in Raleigh. I have a home in a small town just west of Raleigh, in the Carolina foothills."

"What's the name of the town? Maybe I've heard of it."

"I doubt it," she answered wryly. "Cutter's Point, North Carolina. Population just under five thousand. I grew up there."

"Does your family still live there?"

"I have a few cousins still in the area. My father passed away several years ago, and my mother lives in Raleigh now."

"No brothers or sisters?"

"No."

"I see." He looked out the window beside him, obviously trying to think of something else to say.

Kristin realized she was being rude. She had subconsciously started using a tactic she'd learned to discourage annoying conversations—answering questions without elaboration, asking no questions of her own. She had let her worry over her writing and her embarrassment about those unexpected kisses overcome her usual good manners.

"I can't quite place your accent, Perry. You're not originally from New York, are you?"

He seemed relieved that she'd made an effort. He turned back to her with a renewed smile. "I grew up in Denver, but I've traveled quite a bit since I left high school. Earned my undergraduate degree from Stanford, attended Harvard School of Law, taught for a couple of years at Rice University in Houston, and I've traveled from place to place since, working on various political campaigns. I keep an apartment in D.C. now, though I don't spend a lot of time there."

She was almost tempted to ask if he'd ever considered getting a "real" job. But that would be unforgivably rude, even if it was basically what he had asked her earlier. Instead, she asked, "Will you ever run for office yourself?"

"I haven't ruled it out, but I have no plans to do so at this time. To be honest, I think I can make a greater contribution to my party by helping get several of our candidates elected rather than filling an office myself. I have a talent for organizing campaigns. I enjoy it and I've been quite successful with it so far."

"Would you ever run a campaign for someone you don't like or agree with ideologically?"

"Am I for sale to the highest bidder?" His expression remained pleasant, a glint of amusement in his eyes. "No, I'm not. If I don't genuinely support a candidate and consider him—or her—the best qualified choice for the office, I won't take the job."

"You've turned down candidates who've asked for your help?"

"Several times. I believe in what I do, Kristin. It isn't just a job for me."

She still wasn't entirely convinced that Perry wasn't drawn more to the fame and glamour of his career than to any ideological calling, but she merely nodded and murmured something noncommittal. And then she glanced out the window and realized where the driver was taking them. "We're going to the airport?"

Perry's dimples flashed—and her pulse tripped in automatic response. "Yes."

With a stern, silent reprimand to her recalcitrant hormones, she continued evenly, "Will we be getting on an airplane?"

"Yes. That's not a problem for you, is it?"

"I'm not afraid to fly, if that's what you're asking. But where are we going? When will we be back?"

"We'll be back in New York later today," he assured her.

Another, more troublesome question suddenly

occurred to her. "This surprise of yours doesn't involve parachutes, does it?"

He laughed. "No. That was one of the other date packages."

"I know. My mother bought it," Kristin said rather grimly.

Perry looked startled. "Your *mother?*"

"She said it was something she always meant to try."

Perry shook his head. "I'm trying to picture *my* mother jumping out of a plane. I can't see it, unless the plane was in flames and going down."

"Your mother isn't the adventurous type?"

He laughed again. "Hardly. Her idea of high adventure is trying a new restaurant."

"And your father?"

"He does a little fishing. Even catches one occasionally. That, and his business pursuits, are all the adventure he claims to need."

"Do you have brothers or sisters?"

"Two sisters. Both older. Both married, both mothers. Both quite convinced that their younger brother is never going to grow up and settle down."

Kristin was still thinking about that tidbit when Perry ushered her out of the limo and into a beautifully appointed Lear jet.

She could feel her eyes widen as she took in the plush seats and the glossy wood trim inside the airplane. She'd never been on a private jet before—had never flown in anything except a commercial airliner, actually. "Is this yours?"

Perry smiled and shook his head. "No. It belongs

to a friend. He donated its use for today as his contribution to the literacy fund-raiser.''

Kristin noticed that Perry seemed to take the accommodations for granted. He might not own this plane, but it certainly wasn't the first time he'd flown in it, or others like it, perhaps.

She was reminded again of how different Perry Goodman's jet-setting, publicity-seeking routine was from her own quiet, private, often solitary life. Her job involved long hours alone at her computer, with the occasional writers' conference or booksigning or speech to schools and civic clubs thrown in. She'd been interviewed by a few newspapers and had twice appeared on television programs to discuss the romance industry—and to plug her own books, of course. But she'd never hired a publicist, never sought fame or constant attention. All she'd wanted to do was write and have readers enjoy her stories. Being published had been the culmination of her dreams.

She wanted that contentment back.

Reminded yet again of her work, she dug into her purse and pulled out her notebook while Perry went forward to speak with the pilot. She began to describe the interior of the plane in concise phrases. While she was at it, she made a few notations about Perry. She wasn't worried that he would accidentally read her notes—no one could decipher the shorthand she'd developed for research.

Youngest child. Only son, she wrote. *Young prince? Accustomed to attention. Used to having own way. Under pressure from family to settle down?*

All of those observations could be helpful in further developing her hero, Nick O'Donnell, she reflected.

"Writing your will?" Perry dropped into the seat opposite her. "I assure you, this plane is quite safe."

She closed her notebook. "I'm sure it is. Where did you say we're going?"

"I didn't," he reminded her with a chuckle. "But I'll tell you now. We're going to Washington, D.C."

She wasn't particularly surprised by his answer, considering his job. She hadn't been to D.C. since she was a teenager and that had been a school trip. It might be interesting to see it from an insider's point of view. And she could definitely do research while she was there.

Strictly business, she reminded herself with a surreptitious look at her companion. This day was for charity and for research. It was not a date—no matter *what* her mother had said.

PERRY WAS HAVING A LITTLE trouble figuring out Kristin Cole. He had always prided himself on his talent for getting to know people quickly, summing them up after spending only a short time with them. It was one of his strengths as a campaign adviser, clueing his candidates in on the people around them, both opponents and supporters, giving advice about how to handle certain individuals. But darned if he could quite make out what went on inside Kristin's head.

She was certainly pleasant enough during the hours he spent with her. Impeccably polite, if a bit reserved. But she was obviously holding back a great deal about herself. He didn't know her true political affiliations, or how she felt about some of the key issues they heard discussed during their "insider's tour" of Washington, D.C. He didn't know what had made her bid for him at the bachelor auction—or why she'd paid so much to spend time with him, when he thought it was quite glaringly obvious that she wasn't romantically interested in him.

Several times during the day, she pulled a small notebook out of her purse and began to make notes in a shorthand she must have developed on her own. He'd sneaked a few peeks over her shoulder, trying to figure out what she was writing, hoping to discover something, *anything*, about the real Kristin Cole. He couldn't read a word of it.

It was like being on a date with a reporter. No, not a date. That implied something personal. It was more as if he were being interviewed for a feature article—The Life and Times of Perry Goodman.

He'd been followed around by reporters before and he didn't usually mind—after all, getting maximum publicity was one of the goals of his job—but this was different. This wasn't supposed to be an interview. This was supposed to be a date. And yes, maybe his ego was somewhat bruised because Kristin didn't seem to be the least bit attracted to him. With the exception of those two spectacular kisses last night—which had seemed to surprise Kristin even more than him—she had shown little more interest in him than…than in that notebook she kept pulling out.

Had he really become so used to feminine attention? Or was his nose out of joint because this time the attraction seemed to be all one-sided? His side.

He tried to convince himself he was taken with her *because* of her reticence. He'd always had a weakness for a gamble. Though he'd never been tempted by cards or dice, it was the thrill of the challenge—the importance of the stakes—that had drawn him into politics in the first place. And Kristin certainly presented a challenge.

But he knew it was more than that. It was something about her fathomless dark eyes. Or the full curve of her lower lip. Or the poised, almost regal way she held herself, in rather amusing contrast to her diminutive size. Or the way her nose crinkled just a little when she smiled.

He'd worked damned hard for those smiles.

There was something special about Kristin Cole. He just wished he could figure out exactly what it was.

He watched her as the Lear taxied down the runway. She was writing in her notebook again. He was beginning to dislike that notebook in a way that felt almost like jealousy.

He cleared his throat rather loudly, pleased when the noise finally got her attention. She looked up and her gaze locked with his. He gave her a smile he'd worked for years to perfect, and with which he'd had some measure of success in the past.

She studied him a moment, then jotted something down in her notebook.

His smile dimmed. He was beginning to feel uncomfortably like a bug under a microscope. "Making notes for your next novel?"

"Maybe the next one," she agreed. "Or a future

book. I jot down anything I think might be useful, then file the notes away until I need them."

"And what have you found particularly useful today?"

She gave a slight shrug. "Notes about all the fascinating sites you showed me. About what it's like to fly on a private Lear jet. Observations about the political bigwigs we've mingled with today—not specific individuals, of course, just general impressions."

"Am I in your notes?" he asked, trying to give the conversation a personal spin.

What might have been the faintest touch of pink stained her cheeks as she closed her notebook and tucked it into her purse. "I told you, I don't use real people. Only characteristics that intrigue me."

"Oh. And is there anything about me that intrigues you?"

She looked out the window as the plane gathered speed and lifted off the ground. "Remind me to thank our pilot when we get back to New York. Our ride has been very smooth and comfortable so far."

Perry decided to let her get away with the obvious distraction. At least she was talking to him, and not scribbling in her notebook. "When are you going back to North Carolina?"

"In the morning. My flight leaves at nine."

"You said you have a deadline approaching?"

A quick frown crossed her face, almost as if a shadow had passed swiftly in front of her. Her casual tone didn't match her expression. "Yes. I'll have to get back to work as soon as I unpack."

"When is your book due?"

Again, he noticed a flicker of an expression he couldn't quite interpret. "Soon."

"How much do you have left to write?"

"Too much," she said, then laughed as if she'd made a joke.

Perry wasn't so sure she'd been teasing. There was tension in her laughter, a strained quality to her smile. She must be falling a bit behind in her schedule.

"I'm sure you'll manage," he said bracingly, trying to offer encouragement.

For some reason, his words seemed to annoy her more than bolster her. She nodded and looked back out the window.

Perry swallowed a sigh. She'd shut him out again. But he had never been the kind to admit defeat easily. "Was today all work for you, or did you manage to enjoy some of it?"

She looked surprised by his question—and then a bit chagrined. "I enjoyed the day very much," she said, meeting his eyes. "I hope I didn't give you reason to believe otherwise."

"What did you like best?"

"Lunch on Capitol Hill, definitely," she said with a smile.

Encouraged, he nodded. "The food was good, wasn't it?"

"Yes, but it was also very interesting watching all the people."

He remembered that she'd made lots of notes then. Was she ever *not* a writer? Did she ever get so involved in anything that she actually forgot to make notes—either mentally or on paper—to use in some future fictional scene?

He kept her talking about the events of the day during the rest of the flight back to New York. She seemed to be making more of an effort to respond, now that the notebook had been tucked out of sight. Maybe she was finally beginning to relax with him, he thought optimistically. Maybe she simply wasn't comfortable at first with new people—a bit shy, perhaps. He rather fancied that explanation; it gave him a reason to think he didn't have to take her reserve personally—and *that* was a soothing balm to his bruised ego.

As he'd arranged, the limo was waiting at the airport. Perry was pleased that everything had gone according to schedule, with no awkward delays or missed connections. He made a mental note to slip a bonus to his amazingly efficient secretary. Now, if only the rest of the day went as well, he could write this project off as a success—at least as far as his contribution to the literacy fund-raiser was concerned.

"We have dinner reservations at eight," he said once they were on their way to Kristin's hotel. "That gives us time to freshen up and change."

She glanced at her watch and nodded. "That's plenty of time," she agreed. "What shall I wear? Formal or informal?"

"You might want to dress up a bit." He smiled a bit smugly. "Tonight, I've managed to get reservations at..."

His cellular phone chirped, drowning out the name of the exclusive restaurant Perry planned to take her to. Since he'd left instructions that he was not to be disturbed today except for important matters, he sighed and reached for the phone. "Excuse me," he said to Kristin. "This should only take a minute. Hello?"

He knew the moment he heard Marcus's voice that this was, indeed, an important call. It was all Perry could do not to curse when his apologetic aide explained the situation. He had congratulated himself too soon, it seemed. The rest of the date wasn't going to proceed as smoothly as he'd hoped. In fact, it wasn't going to proceed at all.

And just when he'd thought he was finally making headway with Kristin, damn it.

He concluded the call a bit tersely and stowed the small, pager-size phone into its belt-clip holder. "Kristin..."

"You have to cancel dinner, don't you?" There was no accusation in her voice. "I could tell from your tone that something has come up."

He nodded grimly. "I'm really sorry. One of my candidates has gotten himself in a jam in California and I need to get there immediately to handle it."

"Something serious, I take it."

"Yes. A potential scandal. My team swears it's something that has been completely fabricated by the opposition, but I have to check it out for myself before I'm asked for any statements."

"I understand," Kristin assured him, and she certainly seemed to.

"I feel lousy about this. It's not at all the way I wanted our time together to end."

"Please don't worry about it, Perry. I know you have a very hectic schedule."

"Well, yes, but..."

She rested a hand on his arm. "I really do understand."

He looked at her hand. Though the fabric of his shirt lay between her palm and his forearm, he could feel her warmth. Her skin looked very soft, and her fingers were long and delicately shaped. His mind was filled suddenly with an image of that pretty hand stroking his bare skin, her trim, pink nails digging into his back.

He shook his head slightly to banish the pictures, wondering where the hell they'd come from. Whatever had spurred the image, he told himself it had nothing to do with his next words. "I'd like to make this up to you. If you'll give me your home number, I'll call when everything settles down and we can…"

She pulled her hand away, her smile looking a bit forced. "That really isn't necessary. You went to a lot of trouble to entertain me last night and again today. More than I ever expected. You don't owe me anything."

"But…"

The limousine stopped at the front of her hotel. A helpful porter appeared almost immediately to open her door. She scooted toward the opening. "Don't get out. I know you're in a hurry. Good luck with your crisis, Perry. I'm sure if anyone can handle it, you can."

She seemed to be in a hurry to send him on his way. If she was at all disappointed that their date had ended so abruptly, she certainly didn't allow him to see it. His ego took another nosedive. He reached out to catch her arm.

"You'll be hearing from me again, Kristin Cole," he murmured, leaning toward her. Before she could realize his intentions, he covered her mouth with his.

He had wondered if those amazing kisses last night had been a one-time phenomenon. He'd half expected that kissing her again would prove to be just a pleasant diversion—certainly nowhere near as incredible as those first impulsive kisses had been. He'd been quite certain that lightning wouldn't strike twice in this same place in this situation. That his reactions to her last night had been exaggerated by champagne or the fact that they'd been alone outside her room after an evening of romantic music and dancing.

There'd been no champagne today. No tuxedos or evening gowns to create a pretty illusion. Instead of dancing, they'd spent hours sightseeing, "doing the tourist thing," as he'd teasingly referred to it earlier. And they weren't alone now in a softly lit hotel hallway in the middle of the night, but in a limo with a driver behind the wheel, a porter waiting patiently at the door, and a steady flow of people passing outside the car.

And still his head was spinning. Kissing Kristin Cole was a great deal more than a pleasant diversion.

He wasn't sure which of them drew back first. Kristin's eyes were wide and her cheeks bright pink when she slid somewhat clumsily out of the limo, clutching the porter's hand for support. "Goodbye, Perry," she said, her voice sounding high and breathless.

He watched her almost run into the hotel.

No, he thought. Not goodbye. Though she didn't know it yet, he would be seeing her again.

As the limo pulled away from the curb, he found himself wondering if Kristin was even now making notes about their kisses for use in a future love scene.

As the hiccup died away from the girl, he lost himself, wondering if it make was ever now took the notes about their kisses in her in a future type account.

4

KRISTIN WONDERED HOW LONG it would take to learn accounting. Or dentistry. Or maybe she could become a forest ranger. She had to do *something* to support herself now that every ounce of creativity inside her seemed to have dried up.

During the two weeks that had passed since she'd returned home from New York, she had written ten pages...and they were about as exciting as wallpaper paste. She'd spent the first two days writing a character sketch of her hero. Granted, it had been an exercise in procrastination, but she had hoped it would kick-start her writing. She'd drawn heavily on her notes and memories of Perry Goodman, creating a list of potential characteristics that she'd printed out and pinned to the bulletin board next to her computer. That was the last thing she'd accomplished that was even slightly worthwhile.

She'd thought quite a bit about Perry since she'd been home. That was only natural, of course, since she was creating a character loosely based on him. The problem was that her hero wasn't coming to life. He moved through the pages as mechanically as a windup toy. And when she tried to express her equally insipid heroine's instant fascination with the guy, the scenes came out stilted and trite. Kristin felt as though she had forcibly pried every word from her stubborn, uncooperative mind. It was an exhausting and unsatisfying process.

Maybe she should become a firefighter, she mused, lifting her hands from the keyboard to cover her face. She'd always rather liked those shiny red helmets.

Even the videos she always watched when she needed inspiration weren't working for her this time. In the past few days alone, she'd watched *Somewhere in Time, While You Were Sleeping, Titanic, Speed, Ladyhawke*—movies with romantic relationships that usually never failed to motivate her. Love that won out despite the odds, or was found in the most unlikely places. Dashing men and women who were willing to die for each other, if necessary.

But there was no inspiration this time. She simply couldn't re-create that feeling when she sat down to write. Her characters remained flat, their affections for each other tepid. And Kristin was getting very close to throwing her computer out her office window in sheer frustration.

Her telephone rang. She considered letting the machine answer for her. It could be her agent or her editor, and she was in no mood to talk to either of them. Or it might be her mother, rattling on about her scintillating social life—which now included the airline pilot, who'd developed a serious crush on Sophie while dangling from a parachute five thousand feet above solid ground.

Since Kristin had hardly left her house the past two weeks, Sophie was becoming increasingly concerned about her daughter. "How can you find any

inspiration sitting alone inside your office?" she
had asked several times. "You need to get out,
mingle with people, gather ideas. Live a little romance, so it will be easier to write about it."

Though Kristin hadn't said so at the time, she
had begun to worry that the reason she was having
so much trouble writing about love was because
somehow, sometime during the past few months,
she had stopped believing in it. At least for herself.
Of course she hadn't implied such a thing to Sophie, who would have been scandalized at the very
suggestion.

The telephone pealed again—the last ring before
the machine would pick up. Impulsively, Kristin
snatched up the receiver. Any diversion had to be
better than the torment of trying to finish chapter
one. "Hello?"

"Hi, Kristin, it's Maggie. I know you're probably
working and I'm sorry if I've interrupted, but have
you got a minute?"

Kristin had to smile. Maggie Gibson's idea of a
"minute" was usually closer to a half hour or
more—even though she called long-distance from
her home in Illinois. "You know I always have time
for you, Mags. What's up?"

"I'm having trouble with the conflict in my book.
Would you mind doing a little brainstorming with
me? I'll sum up the plot for you and you tell me if
it's as lame as I'm afraid it is."

Kristin didn't know whether to laugh or cry.
This type of call was certainly not unusual between
writers. It was the main reason they so loved getting together at conferences. Theirs was basically
solitary work, and getting together allowed them

to form a network of friends with whom they could whine and share writing-and-publishing "war stories." She'd made many similar calls herself, wanting to get another writer's input on motivation or conflict or pacing or editorial suggestions—and no one understood a writer's problems like another writer.

She hadn't called anyone, however, about the problems she'd been grappling with lately. She wasn't sure that what was wrong with her now could be fixed with a simple phone call. And she still couldn't bring herself to voice the words *writer's block*—or the even worse-sounding phrase, *burned-out*.

"Tell me your plot, Maggie. Let's see if I can find any problems."

Maybe she could help her friend through this relatively minor dilemma—even if she couldn't seem to do anything about her own personal crisis.

PERRY WAS ATTENDING another political fundraiser, this one a $2,500-dollar-a-plate dinner, with the governor of New Jersey as the evening's featured speaker. As was socially expected of him, Perry had brought a date. The whole dating situation was becoming tricky for him these days. If he was seen too often in the company of one particular woman, the gossip mills—and sometimes the woman, herself—read more into it than Perry intended. If he took a different date to every event, he ran the risk of being seen as a "playboy" type, not to be taken seriously.

He'd compromised by cultivating a few good friends who didn't mind being seen at various

functions with him, who wanted nothing more
from him than companionship and an entrée into
his glittering social circles. Elspeth Moore was one
of those generous women. Each time he was photographed with her, they were identified only as
"friends and associates," which suited them both
perfectly.

He took a bite of his dinner and had to make a
massive effort not to shudder. "Yum," he murmured. "Rubber duckie à l'orange. Again."

Elspeth stifled a giggle. "At least you've identified one of the dishes. What's this green glop supposed to be?" she asked in a whisper.

"Puréed tree moss, I believe."

Elspeth's eyes were bright with amusement, but
her carefully trained expression gave no clue to
their impudent conversation. "I can't tell you what
it means to me that you brought me along. I'll certainly try to return the favor. Maybe you'd like to
accompany me to the next ladies' potluck luncheon
I'm invited to attend."

"Green bean casseroles and gelatin molds
stuffed with miniature marshmallows." He gave
her a look. "I'm terribly sorry, Elspeth, but I think
I'm busy that day."

"What a pal." She took a bite of her green glop
and managed a smile as her eyes met those of the
woman across the table. "I'm definitely going to re-
pay you, Perry," she said through her brightly
smiling teeth.

She really was good at this, Perry reflected. The
twenty-six-year-old daughter of a Texas congressman, she'd grown up at affairs like this one. Perry
suspected she had political aspirations of her own.

And he had no doubt that she would achieve them, should she so desire.

More than a few people had suggested that Perry and Elspeth made a good team. Several aspiring matchmakers had given him less-than-subtle nudges in her direction. But Perry and Elspeth remained very good friends. Nothing more.

While Perry had every intention of marrying and starting a family someday—and was well aware that it was time for him to start taking steps in that direction—he couldn't picture himself doing so with Elspeth, no matter how much he liked and admired her. The chemistry simply wasn't there for them. There was no magic.

He almost snorted as he realized where his thoughts had taken him. Chemistry? Magic? Apparently, he'd spent a bit too much time with people in the romance industry lately.

Which, of course, made him think of Kristin Cole, something he'd done quite a bit during the past couple of weeks. He told himself that it was still bothering him that he'd been forced to cut their date short. He'd promised her a special dinner—and then he'd had to dump her at her hotel.

He really should have insisted on walking her up to her room.

She had such beautiful eyes. And without even trying very hard, he could clearly picture that little wrinkle in her nose when she smiled. He wondered if she'd thought about him during the past two weeks, or if she'd happily lost herself in her writing the minute he'd left her sight.

Elspeth had occasionally been accused—only in the nicest way, of course—of being a witch. Perry understood why when she casually asked, "Have you talked to Kristin Cole lately?"

"No," he said, after taking a moment to recover from his surprise that she'd mentioned Kristin just as he was thinking about her. "Not since I had to dump her in New York."

He'd told Elspeth most of what had happened between Kristin and him. He had not, of course, mentioned the kisses that still replayed themselves in his head at awkward moments.

"I liked her."

He nodded and stabbed his fork into a steamed baby carrot. "I liked her, too."

"So call her."

He swallowed the carrot. "Maybe I will."

He didn't add that Kristin hadn't given him her phone number. It was the first time in almost longer than he could remember that any woman had refused to let him know how to reach her. Of course, it had been almost that long since he'd had to ask. He'd had telephone numbers whispered in his ear, scribbled on cocktail napkins, slipped into his pocket—even written on his hand. But Kristin had simply ignored his request.

Elspeth broke into his somber thoughts with a comment. "I read one of her books last week. It was good."

Perry couldn't help chuckling. "You sound surprised."

"I was, a bit. I didn't think a romance novel would be to my taste. But it was really good—just like a real book."

Perry winced, remembering Kristin's reaction

when he'd made a thoughtless comment like that.
"Er—she does write real books, you know."

Elspeth bit her lip. "That was a thoughtless remark, wasn't it? I didn't mean…"

"It's okay. I know what you meant."

"Have you read her work?"

"No," he admitted a bit sheepishly. "Not yet."

He really was going to have to get around to that
soon.

The sudden, piercing shrill of microphone feed-
back made everyone in the room flinch. An embar-
rassed speaker waited until proper sound adjust-
ments had been made, apologized profusely, then
began his long-winded and blatantly obsequious
introductions of the governor, preventing further
conversation among the audience.

Perry tried to pay attention to the speaker, but
his mind kept drifting to a woman in North Carolina. A woman who hadn't given him her number—but who would be hearing from him, anyway.

TWENTY-FOUR HOURS had passed since Kristin had
helped Maggie untangle her plot. Unfortunately,
the brainstorming session hadn't helped Kristin.
She'd written three paragraphs since then—and
she'd deleted all of them.

She had begun to fantasize about selling her
computer and joining the circus.

When her doorbell rang at just after 5:00 p.m.,
she sighed and pushed away from her desk. Probably a delivery, she figured. She was expecting the
line-editing on her last book. Going through the
editorial markings to make sure she agreed with

everything would give her something productive to do with the rest of her evening. And reading her own work would help her remember that she had been a writer once.

She glanced in the hall mirror as she passed. She wasn't exactly looking her best. She'd bundled her hair into a scraggly ponytail and she hadn't bothered with makeup or contact lenses. In addition to her glasses, she was wearing an oversize pink T-shirt beneath baggy denim overalls. Her feet were stuffed into fuzzy Marvin the Martian slippers. The delivery guy had seen her dressed this way before. She wouldn't scare him too badly.

Because she lived in tiny Cutter's Point and hadn't developed the habit, she didn't bother to look through the window before she opened the door. Which meant that she was in total open-mouthed shock when she discovered Perry Goodman on her doorstep where she'd expected to find a delivery driver.

Wearing a sharply tailored suit, he looked as drop-dead gorgeous as she remembered. And he was looking at her as though he'd never seen her before.

Resisting an impulse to lift a hand to her messy ponytail, she placed it on her hip, instead. "Perry Goodman. This is a surprise."

He recovered swiftly from his initial double-take. "Hello, Kristin."

"You, uh, just happened to be passing through town?"

"No. I came specifically to see you. I'd have called first, but you neglected to give me your phone number." His smile was a bit smug.

She hadn't given him her address, either. Since both of them were aware of that, she saw no need to mention it. She stepped out of the doorway, knowing—as he must have known—that she wouldn't turn him away. "Come in."

"Thank you." He stepped past her, into the living room.

Fortunately, she'd had a housecleaning binge the day before, after talking to Maggie. It had been another way to distract herself from writing, but at least the place was clean.

"Nice house," Perry commented, studying her simple Shaker furniture and the bright splashes of color she had added.

"Thank you."

He examined a framed photograph on the mantel. "Is this your mother?"

"Yes."

"I think I saw her at the bachelor auction."

"My mother's rather hard to miss. Sit down, Perry. Can I get you anything?"

"Not just now, thank you," he said. He waited until she was seated before he settled onto the couch. "How have you been?"

It was so surreal that he was sitting on her couch making small talk. She'd seen him on CNN just that very morning. She made an effort to answer as casually as he'd asked. "Fine, thank you. Um, why are you here?"

He smiled. "I owe you a dinner, remember? I always pay my debts."

She couldn't believe he'd done this. She hadn't expected to ever see him again—off the television screen, anyway. Maybe she should be annoyed that he'd arrogantly shown up without a call, confident of his welcome. But she wasn't really annoyed.

Although she should probably be a bit nervous about his motives in tracking her down this way. But, she thought, as she eyed his pleasant smile and relaxed posture, she knew she had nothing to fear from Perry Goodman. Nothing like that, anyway.

She supposed some people would be flattered that he'd made the effort to find her again. And maybe she was—a little. She just didn't know what to do about it.

She decided to try to handle it with humor. "And did you bring it with you?"

"Dinner?" He smiled. "No. We'll have to go out for it."

"Did you ever consider that I might have other plans for the evening?"

"Of course. I'm perfectly willing to wait until you're free."

"And if that's not until sometime next week?"

He chuckled. "Then I suppose I'll have to leave town and come back. Maybe we should pull out our calendars?"

Making a quick decision, she shook her head. "That won't be necessary. As it happens, I have no plans for this evening."

It would have been nice if he'd pretended to be surprised. Instead, he only nodded with some satisfaction and said, "Great. Let's make it tonight, then."

"Fine," she said. After all, he'd come all this way just to make it up to her that he'd had to cancel the last part of their arranged date. It really had been very nice of him, even if he *should* have called first. She suspected that her reluctance to give him her phone number had piqued his ego a bit, and this had been his subtle way of repaying her. She imagined that most single women—and maybe a few who weren't single—would beg him to call them. "You'll have to give me time to change."

He nodded. "Would you mind if I wait here while you do? I won't get in your way. I can watch the news or something."

Because it was going to take her a while to get presentable, she decided she'd better get started. She stood, tugging the rubber band out of her ponytail and feeling her hair tumble to her shoulders. "The television's behind that cabinet door, along with the remote control. There are sodas and fruit juices in the refrigerator, glasses in the cabinet to the right. If you want a snack, there are some homemade oatmeal-raisin cookies in the Marvin the Martian cookie jar on the kitchen counter. Make yourself at home. I'll try to hurry."

"Take your time. I'll be fine."

Kristin hesitated only a moment before she nodded and walked into her bedroom, closing the door behind her. And then she opened her closet door and stared into it, trying to concentrate on what to wear instead of the man who was making himself at home in her living room.

RESTLESS BY NATURE—not to mention curious— Perry paced the living room after helping himself to a soda and a couple of cookies from the kitchen. He studied the titles of books in the many bookshelves, looked at photographs, examined a whimsical collection of knickknacks. He gazed out the window that overlooked a pretty vista of moonwashed trees and hills and a glitter of what might have been water. Kristin's house, he'd discovered earlier, sat right on the edge of a small lake. He imagined the scenery from her windows was particularly beautiful in the daytime. Maybe she'd chosen to live here just so that view could relax her and put her in the mood to write.

And then his pacing led him to an open door of a room that obviously served as Kristin's office.

Remembering that she'd told him to make himself at home—and knowing full well her invitation hadn't extended quite this far—he entered the room. Nice computer system, he thought. Marvin the Martian, again, this time on a mouse pad. She had a scanner. Two printers—one laser for black-and-white copies, another smaller one for color printing. A fax machine. A copy machine. Stereo system and small TV with built-in VCR.

Kristin shared his appreciation for electronic toys, he thought with a smile.

A bookshelf next to a large file cabinet held a neat row of books with Kristin's name printed on the spine, some translated into several other languages, he noted with interest. The lower shelves were stuffed with reference books. Dictionaries. Thesauruses. Atlases. A couple of medical dictionaries. Books of quotations. Others he didn't recognize.

Post-it notes in a dizzying array of colors were stuck haphazardly on nearly everything in the room. Some of them contained scribbled messages in that weird shorthand he remembered from before. Others held dates and numbers. Deadlines, perhaps? Page counts? He shrugged and moved on.

A bulletin board took up a large portion of the wall next to her desk. Several pictures, cut or torn from magazines and catalogs, were pinned to it. Was this how she kept her character descriptions in mind? Did she describe the faces exactly, or just use certain attributes, the way she said she used isolated characteristics of people she met? He was beginning to find the process of her work interesting, evoking questions he'd never really considered before.

Two sheets of paper were also pinned to the bulletin board. Each bore a heading above what appeared to be lists of phrases. "Character sketch— Amy Hulsizer," he read at the top of the first page. And on the other—"Character sketch—Nick O'Donnell."

The main characters in the book she was writing? He thought they would be referred to as the hero and heroine. Was this how she brought her characters to life in her own mind before attempting to do so for her readers? He wondered if she had made these lists before or after their date. If it had been after, would he recognize any characteristics from people they'd met during the time they'd spent together? Would he recognize any of his own?

Naturally, he couldn't resist reading the character sketch of her hero. "Only son," he noted on the first line, and he smiled. "Two older sisters."

Apparently he'd made a pretty good impression on her, after all, he thought, his formerly deflated ego swelling a bit. She was using him for her hero. But as he read on, his smile faded into a scowl.

5

KRISTIN DIDN'T LINGER LONGER than necessary over her appearance, but it took a little more than half an hour for her to shower, do her hair, put on a touch of makeup and get dressed. She slipped into a short-sleeved mint-green cardigan and a long floral skirt in mint, pink and lavender, sliding her feet into fashionably thick-soled slides. It was a less-sophisticated ensemble than the ones she'd worn with Perry before, but this wasn't New York or Washington, D.C. This was the way she dressed in her "real" life.

She found Perry sitting on the couch where she had left him. He was watching a news wrap-up on CNN and talking on his cell phone. Was he ever not on the job? And, as busy as he always was, why had he come all the way here just to take her to dinner? Was it really only because he had such a highly developed sense of responsibility? Or was he concerned that she would say something less than flattering about the cut-short date package, putting him in a bad light in regard to the high-profile charity project?

A politician, she reminded herself, was always concerned with image, even when his role in politics was primarily behind the scenes.

She stayed back until he'd concluded the call,

then stepped into his line of vision. "I hope I didn't keep you waiting too long."

"Not at all," he assured her, rising automatically to his feet, demonstrating the impeccable manners she'd noticed from him before. Not counting the way he'd shown up on her doorstep without calling first, of course. "You look very nice."

"Thank you." She studied his bland smile for a moment. Something about him had changed in the half hour she'd left him alone. Something in his eyes, perhaps.

She shook her head slightly, telling herself she was being overly imaginative. Unless…she nodded toward the phone he still held in his hand. "Has something come up?"

"Am I about to cancel on you again? Absolutely not." He slipped the phone into its holder. "I was just taking care of a little business while you got ready. I'm free now."

She nodded, telling herself again that she must have been imagining undercurrents that simply weren't there.

Perry motioned toward the door. "Are you ready to go eat?"

"As a matter of fact, I'm starving," she answered candidly. "I only had an apple and a diet soda for lunch."

He chuckled and moved toward the door. "Then, by all means, let's go feed you. I would hate to be accused of being too self-absorbed to take care of a starving woman."

Though his tone was teasing, something in it made Kristin hesitate. Just what had he meant by *that* comment? She looked at him questioningly, noting that, while his smile was relaxed and pleasant, his eyes were shuttered. Unreadable. For the first time since she had met him, he made her a little nervous.

The moment passed so quickly, she wondered if she'd been letting her imagination run away with her again. Perry looked perfectly at ease when he opened the door and made a teasing bow. "After you, ma'am."

Maybe her brains were still addled from the surprise of seeing him again. Maybe that was why she kept imagining that beneath his sexy smiles, Perry Goodman was more than a little annoyed with her. Since she could think of nothing she had done to deserve that, she merely smiled and swept past him. "Why, thank you, sir."

"You obviously know the area better than I do," he said when they were belted into his car. "Where's the nicest place to eat in town?"

She couldn't help giggling. "If you want a nice restaurant, we'll have to go into Raleigh. Cutter's Point isn't exactly known for its gourmet cuisine."

"I liked what I saw of your town as I drove in. The little town square I passed, with its old buildings and flowering gardens. The neighborhoods like this one. Front porch swings that look as though folks actually sit out on them on nice evenings and visit with their neighbors. There's a definite appeal in that sort of town for someone who spends entirely too much time in big cities."

She sighed, his words filling her with nostalgia. "Even here, the lazy evenings on porch swings are becoming less common. Everyone's always so busy. Rushing to jobs in Raleigh or other neighboring cities. Taking their kids to soccer or softball practice, dance lessons, karate lessons or to the malls in Raleigh to buy the latest designer labels, which have invaded even our little schools. A lot of the residents here enjoy the old-fashioned ambience of Cutter's Point but find themselves involved in the rat race, despite themselves."

"You're destroying all my illusions about small-town life," he complained.

"Sorry. You'd get a few of them back if we stay in town to eat. In Cutter's Point, we have a choice of the Main Street Diner—where tonight's special is chicken-fried steak with cream gravy—or Big Bubba's Hubcap Burgers."

Perry laughed. "Unless you have a serious craving for either of those delightful places, maybe we'll just drive into Raleigh."

"Good choice," she assured him.

At Perry's urging, Kristin selected one of her favorite places, an upscale restaurant with an eclectic menu and an intimate, very comfortable atmosphere. No reservations were accepted, and there was usually a brief wait for a table, but patrons rarely minded waiting in the cheerful bar where talented local jazz bands played from a small stage.

Perry seemed to approve of her choice. He complimented the music they heard as they sipped white wine before dinner, and commented on the clever decor throughout the establishment. After being led to a table some twenty minutes after their arrival, he studied the menu with interest. "Fascinating," he murmured.

"The management takes pride in presenting dishes that aren't widely available elsewhere in this region," she informed him, pleased that she seemed to have chosen well.

"No kidding. I'm having trouble deciding what to try."

"My mother highly recommends the ostrich. I usually select from the seafood dishes. I love seafood."

"Your mother sounds like an interesting woman."

"She is definitely...different."

Perry closed his menu and set it aside. "And what about you? Are you 'different'?"

She shrugged and kept her eyes on the menu. "That depends on who you ask, I suppose. I tend to think of myself as rather ordinary."

"Most of the writers I've met have considered themselves a bit eccentric. The moody, artistic types. You don't have any creative quirks?"

"I suppose I have my share." She was a bit relieved when a waiter arrived to take their orders. She'd never been comfortable dissecting her own psyche—artistic or otherwise.

After placing their orders, they studied each other across the table again. Since Perry seemed in no hurry to break the silence, Kristin felt compelled to do so. "You decided to trust my mother's judgment?"

He nodded. "I haven't had ostrich in a while. It should make a nice change from all the 'rubber chicken' dinners I've eaten lately."

"It always seems to surprise first-timers that ostrich tastes more like beef than chicken or turkey," she commented, simply to make conversation.

"You said you grew up in this area. Have you ever lived anywhere else?"

"I moved to Florida after I graduated from high school. I earned my degree at Florida State, then lived in Tampa for nearly four years. I moved back to Cutter's Point after I sold my second book."

"Why?"

"Why, what?"

"Why do you choose to live in such a small town? Wouldn't it be more convenient for you, careerwise, to live in New York?"

She shrugged. "I work with my editor by phone and fax, anyway. And I see my agent as often as necessary, which is only once or twice a year. I like the peace and quiet of Cutter's Point."

"Still, I would think the social opportunities would be rather limited."

She smiled wryly. "I manage to entertain myself."

"Is there a special man in your life who helps to keep you entertained?" he asked a bit too casually.

She lifted an eyebrow and answered succinctly. "No."

"Still looking for one of those romance heroes, hmm?"

Kristin frowned. Something was definitely bugging him. What had she done to irk him? "I'm not necessarily looking for anyone. I'm perfectly happy with my life as it is."

It was a good thing, she thought, that her meal hadn't been served yet. She might well have choked on that lie. But it wasn't her lack of a love life that was bothering her—not entirely, anyway. It was the difficulty she was having with her career—something she had no intention of discussing with Perry.

"So you don't believe the guys in your books really exist? Those larger-than-life heroes who sweep the women off their feet and carry them away to live happily ever after?"

She phrased her answer carefully. "I certainly believe in happy endings, if you're referring to successful marriages. I've seen many examples among my friends and relatives. And if you'd ever actually read one of my books, you would know that the heroes I create may be larger than life in some ways, but they also have very human flaws and vulnerabilities. Personal growth is part of the journey my characters undertake—they have to overcome their own problems, find their own fulfillment, before they are free to love each other fully. The women aren't 'carried away' to find happiness. They find it for themselves."

"In other words, they don't need a man."

She frowned. "They hope to find love, of course. Someone to share their lives with. Children. But they are capable of taking care of themselves."

"And how much are your heroines like you?"

Again, Kristin was relieved when their conversation was interrupted. She kept her eyes on the table while their meals were placed in front of them, wondering how she could change the subject without being overly obvious. She didn't usually mind talking about her work, but it was making her uncomfortable this evening. Mostly, of course, because her writing was giving her so much grief lately. But it was also because of Perry's enigmatic undertone—that funny feeling that there were rea-

sons for his questions she couldn't quite understand.

Fortunately, Perry seemed to sense her reluctance to continue their former conversation. They
made small talk during dinner, Perry entertaining
her with anecdotes about funny things that had
happened to him on the campaign trail. He was
quite amusing when he chose to be, and she found
herself laughing out loud a time or two. He was
most definitely a charmer, and she could enjoy his
company—as long as he wasn't delving into areas
that were too painful to talk about at the moment.
And as long as she kept in mind that charm was no
indication of what lay beneath it.

"You lead a very exciting life," she commented
as they ate. "You must enjoy traveling and being
around people."

"Most of the time. There are times, however,
when I crave peace and quiet. Solitude. That's
when I head for an island somewhere to chill out
for a few days."

"Do you get the chance to do that very often?"

"A couple of times a year. That's all I usually
need to recharge."

She chuckled as an ironic thought occurred to
her.

"What's so funny?"

She wrinkled her nose. "I was just thinking that
you and I lead almost opposite lives. Your job is
very public, and you look for quiet and solitude
when you vacation. I work in isolation, and I usually go to crowded conferences or to bustling cities
for vacations. It just struck me as amusing."

Perry didn't seem to find her observation quite

so funny. "There are things about our jobs that are similar. We both need promotion and publicity to get our products—your books and my clients—visible in the market. We both make our living by selling our ideas, which we hope will appeal to a large audience."

"I hadn't thought of it quite that way."

Looking rather pleased with himself, he nodded. "I just thought I should point out that I'm not the only one who requires public attention to be successful at what I do."

"Did I sound critical of your work?" she asked curiously. "If I did, it was unintentional. I said our lives are different, but I certainly wasn't making a judgment of one being better than the other. Just…different."

"So you *don't* think I'm a shallow, publicity-hungry media hound?"

There was definitely a note of challenge in his voice this time. She was almost certain she wasn't imagining it. She must have said or done something to make him feel that she'd been judging him. She wished she knew what it was.

She phrased her reply carefully. "Obviously, I don't know you very well, since we've only spent a few hours together. From what I've seen, you are both successful and happy in your career, and you seem to be quite popular among your associates. You've gone out of your way to be nice to me, and I admire the generous contribution of time and expense you gave to the literacy project. If you're asking if my opinion of you has been generally positive during the short time we've known each other, the answer is yes."

He laughed softly, ruefully, shaking his head. "Spoken like a consummate politician. If you ever decide to run for an office, let me know. It makes my job so much easier when my candidate knows how to answer questions with such tact."

"You confuse me, Perry," she confessed after a pause, wishing she knew just what was going on inside his head.

His left eyebrow shot up in an ironic expression. "That's only fair," he murmured, "because you have me totally baffled, Kristin Cole."

She felt her eyes go wide with surprise. "I do?"

"Yes."

"Why?"

"I haven't quite been able to figure you out yet. But," he added, breaking into his patented, dimple-bracketed smile, "I haven't stopped trying."

Kristin cleared her throat. Something in his eyes made her nervous—as if he'd just issued a challenge she didn't quite know how to prepare for. She turned her attention to finishing her meal, telling herself she was being fanciful again. Perry had come to town only to tie up the loose ends of their charity date. If he'd had something more in mind—and if that hadn't changed during dinner—she would have to find a way to let him know there was no need to waste his time and charm.

Regardless of all the "opposites attract" stories she'd read and written, she and Perry were the most unlikely match she could imagine. And this was the absolute worst time for her to even consider getting involved with anyone. She was so distraught about her career and still smarting so badly over her last broken relationship that she simply couldn't trust her own judgment. She needed time, and she needed to rebuild her confidence, in several areas.

She couldn't allow herself to be distracted from that by another romance that seemed destined to end in heartache. No matter how delectable Perry Goodman looked when he smiled. No matter how appealing his dimples were. No matter how flattered she was that he'd gone to so much trouble to complete their interrupted date. No matter how many times she had replayed his kisses and tried—unsuccessfully—to convince herself they hadn't really been the most spectacular kisses she'd ever experienced.

She peeked up from her meal to glance at him again. He was watching her, his dimples very much in evidence, his eyes warm enough to bring a faint flush of heat to her cheeks.

Okay, she thought with a silent gulp, so they *had* been amazing kisses. And, okay, so she wouldn't mind sampling a few more of them. But she was strong enough to resist temptation when she knew it would only lead to regret.

At least, she hoped she was....

KRISTIN COLE FRUSTRATED Perry more than any woman he'd met in a very long time. He'd gone out of his way to charm her. How long had it been since he'd tried so hard—and since he'd had so little reward for his efforts?

Though she was pleasant-enough company, he still had the feeling that Kristin thought of him only as a diversion. If there was any sexual attraction on her part, she did a darned good job of concealing it. If she even remembered that he'd kissed her, it certainly didn't show in her unreadable dark eyes when she studied him across the table.

Perry, on the other hand, had given a great deal of thought to those kisses. Wondering what the chances were that there would be more of them.

He had an uncomfortable suspicion that Kristin didn't actually like him very much. He didn't know why—he'd been on his very best behavior for her. Without undue vanity, he was aware that most people, particularly women, liked him—with the exception, of course, of political opponents. And several of *them* had admitted that they would like him very well if he was on their side.

Having grown accustomed to being the object of attention—and, okay, maybe more than a little spoiled by the adulation—Perry was having trouble resigning himself to giving up on Kristin. He liked her—why didn't she reciprocate?

He thought of that character sketch he'd spied in her office. He'd thought at first she'd used him as a model for her hero, and he'd found that encouraging. But then he'd read on, finding words like *cocky*, *self-absorbed* and *attention hungry* on the list—and he'd hoped she'd written that list long before she met him.

But he still had a sneaky, uncomfortable suspicion that he *was* the model for her character…and that all those words described the way she saw him. How could he change her mind? And why was it becoming so important for him to try, when she'd given him so little encouragement? He'd never considered himself a glutton for punishment before.

Kristin initially hesitated about ordering dessert, but Perry urged her to indulge. "You said you had a light lunch."

"True," she said, visibly wavering. And then she capitulated. "They serve a wonderful key lime pie here. I'll have that."

"Sounds great." Perry set his dessert menu aside and smiled at the waitress. "Make it two. I love key lime pie."

The waitress returned his smile, a hint of flirtation in her voice when she replied, "I'll make sure you get an extra-large slice, then."

Kristin lifted an eyebrow as the waitress sashayed away. "Looks as though you've made another fan."

He frowned. Just what did she mean by that? Was it another subtle dig? Or just an innocuous, teasing remark? He remembered something else he'd read on the character sketch for Nick O'Donnell. "Somewhat conceited. Accustomed to feminine attention."

Did Kristin see him that way? Or, again, was he only imagining that Nick O'Donnell had been based on himself?

Before he could decide how to respond, her attention had already wandered. He followed her gaze and spotted an older couple across the room, holding hands on top of their little table and gazing at each other with soft, sweet smiles.

"They must be celebrating an anniversary," he murmured, latching onto a subject he thought would appeal to Kristin. "Their fiftieth, maybe?"

Still watching the other table, she shook her

head. "He just gave her an engagement ring. She's
wearing it now."

Perry glanced over his shoulder again, noticing
the diamond glittering on the woman's time-
weathered left hand. The pair had to be in their
seventies, but they were gazing at each other like
love-struck teenagers. Perry smiled and turned
back to his own companion. Only to feel his smile
fade when he spotted the dreaded notebook again.
She'd pulled it out of her purse and was scribbling
away rapidly. Were all writers so constantly on the
lookout for usable tableaux?

She set the notebook aside when the waitress delivered their desserts. Perry's was at least twice the
size of Kristin's, and delivered with a giggle. Kristin gave him a wry look. Perry felt his cheeks
warm. It wasn't as if he'd actively flirted with the
waitress. He'd simply been nice to her. Other
women responded to him—why didn't Kristin?

Maybe he was being too subtle.

He took a bite of his pie. "Mmm. Tart, tasty and
tempting. Like you," he added with a lift of his
eyebrows.

She looked at him as if he'd just pulled a quarter
from his ear. "Do you have much luck with that
line?"

"On occasion," he answered ruefully. *So much
for that approach.*

Kristin nodded thoughtfully and made another
notation in her notebook.

As much as he hated losing, Perry wondered if it
was time to concede defeat in his campaign to win
Kristin Cole's approval.

Optimist that he was, Perry chose to believe he'd

made headway with Kristin during dessert. The treat served to put her in a mellow mood, and she even laughed aloud at a couple of his jokes.

Damn, but that little crinkle in her nose made him crazy. And the way her dark eyes sparkled when she laughed. And the slightest hint of a dimple just at the right corner of her mouth.

Maybe he wouldn't concede defeat just yet, after all. Maybe she was just a little shy—a little slow to warm up to new guys.

She finally declared herself unable to eat another bite. "That really was a wonderful meal," she said with a satisfied sigh. "Much better than the canned soup or cold sandwich I probably would have made for myself."

"I enjoyed it, too. But that was due as much to the company as to the food."

"You're flirting again."

"A little," he admitted. "Do you want me to stop?"

"I suppose a little flirting never hurt anyone," she said after a moment, her tone just coy enough to give him a bit more encouragement.

Perry paid for the meal, then escorted Kristin out to his rented car. He rested his hand at the small of her back as they crossed the parking lot. It rather amused him that he felt almost like a teenager again, smugly pleased that he'd found the courage to touch her—and that she was allowing him to do so.

He tuned the radio to soft, sultry music for the drive back to her house, leaving the volume low and intimate. He was already anticipating being alone with her again. Remembering the way she'd responded when he'd kissed her before, he couldn't help wondering what she would do if—when—he kissed her again.

It seemed quite natural when she turned to him at her door and said, "Would you like to come in for coffee?"

"I'd love to," he answered promptly. Things were definitely looking up.

He followed her into her kitchen, deliberately not looking at her office as he passed the open door. Leaning against a counter, he watched her as she prepared the coffee. "I like your kitchen."

He'd admired it earlier while she'd changed for dinner. The kitchen had a comfortable, homey feel to it—dark oak cabinets, green granite countertops, wood floor, copper-bottomed pans and green plants in wicker baskets. Another wicker basket sat close to his elbow, filled with envelopes, coupons and scraps of paper. He could picture Kristin sitting at the island bar in this comfortable room with her coffee, reading the newspaper or her mail, watching the small television on the counter.

He could almost picture himself breakfasting with her.

"Thank you." She pulled two mugs out of a cabinet. "Do you take anything in your coffee?"

"No, just black. Do you like to cook?"

"I rarely go to the trouble just for myself, but I enjoy hosting the occasional dinner party."

"What's your specialty?"

"Pasta dishes, mostly. They're easy, healthy and very versatile."

"I love pasta, any way it's prepared."

Kristin turned to lean back against the counter

behind her while they waited for the coffee to brew. "Do *you* like to cook?"

"I've never learned," he admitted. "It's something I've meant to try, but I never seem to find the time. I can scramble eggs, grill cheese and nuke a few things, but that's pretty much the extent of my culinary repertoire."

"Cooking is really not that hard. It's simply a matter of following written directions."

"Maybe you could help me cook something sometime."

"Maybe," she agreed.

Did he hear doubt in her voice? And if so, was it because she found it unlikely that they would share a cooking lesson—or that they would even see each other again?

If she thought he was only making polite conversation, that he had no interest in seeing her again after this evening ended, then she was mistaken. He hadn't come to Cutter's Point to fulfill an obligation—not primarily, anyway. He'd come because he'd wanted to see Kristin again. And he already suspected he would want to see her again after tonight.

He just wasn't at all sure she felt the same way. And, again, he was struck by how unusual it was for him to be so uncertain about a woman's interest.

Perry wasn't the type to hesitate for long. His see-the-hill, take-the-hill attitude had carried him a long way in his career and had occasionally spilled over into his personal life. He called on that determination now as he straightened away from the counter and took a step toward Kristin. "There's something I've been wanting to do all evening."

It was obvious that she didn't need to ask what he meant. She held up a hand, palm toward him, a gesture of warning. "Perry..."

"Kristin," he cut in, moving relentlessly forward. "Have I mentioned that you have the cutest nose I've ever seen?"

She blinked. "Er...my nose?"

"Yeah. Cute as all-get-out, as my grandmother used to say." He took the final step toward her. The hand she'd extended to stop him ended up resting against his chest.

Kristin recovered very quickly from her momentary discomfiture. "Nevertheless..."

He was amused by her wording. "I also have a thing for your mouth. That adorable almost-dimple at the right corner makes me just itch to taste it."

A wave of pink washed across her cheeks. She made a visible effort to speak firmly. "I know I said earlier that I didn't mind a little flirtation, but..."

He shook his head. "I was indulging in 'a little flirtation' at dinner. This is something different."

She hadn't removed her hand from his chest. Her fingers flexed against the fabric of his shirt. "You're confusing me again," she complained.

He smiled and lowered his head. "Good," he murmured. And covered her mouth with his.

His final coherent thought was that he was glad she hadn't pushed him away—that she was, in fact, kissing him back. And then her lips parted softly beneath his and he couldn't think at all.

6

PERRY DIDN'T UNDERSTAND what happened when he kissed Kristin Cole. He didn't hear bells or music or fireworks—exactly. The ground didn't shift beneath his feet, nor the world tilt on its axis. But there was definitely something different about her kisses. Something that could all too easily become addictive.

After a long, very pleasant interlude, Kristin seemed to suddenly realize what she was doing. She pulled back with a gasp. "The, uh…the coffee's ready," she said, as if that announcement were supremely important.

"It can wait," he replied, and pulled her back into his arms.

With a little murmur of what might have been resignation, she wrapped her arms around his neck and lifted her face to his. Perry had to forcibly restrain himself from devouring her. Her lips were so soft, her mouth so sweet. She was warm and vibrant in his arms, her curves seemingly tailored to his hands. She made a muffled sound of pleasure when he stroked his palms from her shoulder blades to her hips.

Maybe, he thought, she was beginning to like him after all.

Lack of oxygen finally forced him to raise his

head. "If you knew how often I've thought of kissing you during the past two weeks..." he murmured, then proceeded to do so again.

It was Kristin who drew back the next time, taking a deep, shaky breath. "This really isn't a good idea," she said, her voice low and unsteady.

He nuzzled against her temple. "Then why does it feel so good?"

Her neck arched when his lips touched the soft spot just in front of her ear. She liked that, he thought with satisfaction.

There was a new, husky edge to her voice when she spoke again. "We hardly know each other."

He kissed her ear again and smiled when a shiver betrayed her. "I think we're getting to know each other pretty well."

"This is not the way I usually get to know someone."

He noticed that she didn't remove her arms from around his neck. He lowered his head again and spoke against her lips. "Maybe, just this once, you could make an exception."

She murmured something incoherent into his mouth. He hoped she was agreeing with him. She certainly felt agreeable as she moved even more closely against him, her breasts pressing against his chest.

Yielding to temptation, he slid his hand from her hip upward, his palm itching with impatience to feel her softness. And then his elbow bumped the shallow wicker basket he'd noticed earlier, the one filled with envelopes and papers. The basket tumbled off the counter, spilling its contents around their feet.

Slick move, Goodman, he thought in disgust as Kristin pushed away from him. Why was it that things always went wrong when he was around Kristin?

"I'm sorry," he said, kneeling to help her gather the contents of the fallen basket. "I'm not usually quite so clumsy."

"I'm sure you're not," she said, sounding amused as she reached for a twenty-cents-off coupon for grape jelly.

Perry pulled a scrap of paper from beneath the dishwasher, his mouth twisting as he recognized Kristin's illegible shorthand. For all he knew, it was a note about what a geek he was.

An envelope had fallen behind him, its contents spread around it. Photographs, he noticed as he gathered them up. Kristin was in most of them, and she looked so pretty he couldn't help but stop and admire them. She'd been wearing denim shorts that showed her legs to their best advantage, and a sleeveless top that made the most of her curves. Her hair was down to her shoulders and gleamed in the sunlight. The photos seemed to have been taken at an amusement park. In several of them, Kristin was shown with a towheaded little girl of perhaps seven or eight. In others, she stood by a good-looking, sandy-haired guy who usually had an arm around her.

They looked, Perry thought grimly, like a very happy family.

Kristin reached for the photos. "I'll put those back in the envelope."

"Looks like you were having a good time," he

commented, wondering how to ask who the man and child were and what they meant to Kristin.

"My mother took those last summer. We were at an amusement park with some…friends." Her expression was pensive as she looked down at a picture of herself standing between the man and the child, all of them laughing, their arms entwined.

Perry wondered what had happened to make her so sad when she looked at the photographs. It was all he could do not to ask all the questions swirling in his head. There were so many things he wanted to know about Kristin—everything, actually. Not the least of which was what it would be like when they finally made love. He deliberately used the word *when* rather than *if*, hoping positive thinking would pay off.

He looked back down at his feet, finding one remaining photograph facedown on the floor. He picked it up and turned it over. The image made him scowl. Kristin and the man from the other pictures had been captured in an embrace, her arms around his neck, their faces very close together, obviously the prelude to a kiss. And Perry found himself fighting an unexpected surge of sheer masculine possessiveness, an uncharacteristic impulse to bash the guy's teeth in.

"Here's another," he said, extending it toward Kristin.

She took it without looking at him. She gave only a glance to the photograph before stuffing it into the envelope with the others. "That looks like everything," she said, straightening to set the basket back on the counter.

Perry rose to his feet. "Kristin—"

Still refusing to meet his eyes, she stepped far out of his reach. "It's getting late," she said with a meaningful look at the wall clock. "Do you still want your coffee before you go?"

That had been about as subtle as a sledgehammer. She'd offered coffee, so she would give him coffee. But then she would show him the door.

Something told him there would be little he could do or say to change her mind tonight. The mood had been broken and her defenses were firmly back in place. And he'd have to be an idiot not to know that it had something to do with the man in those photographs.

He needed to think about this. To decide what his next step should be—and to try to figure out whether he truly wanted to take that step. "It is getting late," he said, looking automatically at his watch. "Maybe I'd better skip the coffee tonight."

She seemed concerned that she'd broken some rule of etiquette. "You're sure you won't have a cup before you go?"

"Thanks, but I'm sure." He knew if he didn't leave now, he was only going to try to kiss her again. Or more. Unless he wanted to lose whatever headway he'd made with her, it would be better if he removed himself from temptation.

She walked him to the door. "Do you have a place to stay tonight?"

"I'm staying in a hotel close to the airport in Raleigh. I have an early flight tomorrow. I have to be in D.C. for a luncheon."

It would have been nice if she'd looked just a little disappointed that he was leaving town. But she only nodded. "Have a safe trip."

He turned to her at the door. "There's just one thing I need to know before I leave."

She looked at him a bit doubtfully. "What is it?"

He kept his eyes focused intently on her face as he asked, "Are you still in love with him?"

For a moment, he thought she wasn't going to answer. And then she shook her head. "No."

The certainty of the single-word response encouraged him. Gave him the courage to lean down and brush a kiss across her cheek. "Then you'll be hearing from me."

She stood very still as he opened the door and stepped outside. He was almost to his car when she called after him. "Perry?"

He turned to find her standing in her doorway, wringing her hands. "Yes?"

"My new book…it isn't going very well."

"I'm sorry to hear that." He waited, knowing there would be more.

"And I really don't like politics. I'm afraid it bores me."

He wasn't particularly surprised by that revelation. And since this was hardly the time to go into a dissertation about why every citizen should be interested in politics, he merely nodded and said, "Okay."

He didn't seem to be reacting the way she expected him to. She continued doggedly. "Perry, this is a really bad time for me. And even if it wasn't, you and I really don't have much in common."

"I'm not so sure about that. We'll compare notes next time and see how many things we both like."

"Next time? I just told you…"

"Good night, Kristin. You'll be hearing from me." He climbed quickly into his car before she could say something he really didn't want to hear. She was still standing in her doorway when he drove away.

SOMETIMES WHEN KRISTIN had trouble being creative at the computer, she took a thick pad of unlined paper, a brand new rollerball pen and a glass of iced tea out to her deck. There she could watch the birds and squirrels playing in the trees, and enjoy the small slice of glittering blue lake she could see from her place—as close to lakefront property as she'd been able to afford when she'd bought her house. She would sit in one of her wrought-iron spring rockers, her feet propped in front of her, and the words would often just seem to flow onto the paper.

After sitting on the deck for more than an hour on this particular afternoon, there were only two words on the paper in front of her. *Perry Goodman.*

She ripped the page from the pad and, crumpling it into a ball, threw it to the other side of the deck. "This," she said aloud, startling a sparrow that had been exploring the deck rail, "is ridiculous."

It had been two days since Perry's visit, and Kristin had been spending entirely too much time since then thinking about him and wondering when she would hear from him again. Not if, but when. He'd made it quite clear that he would be calling again.

She'd tried not to encourage him to expect anything to happen between them. She was honest enough to acknowledge that a certain chemistry existed between them—okay, there was a *lot* of chemistry between them, as evidenced by the volatile reactions every time they kissed. She had little doubt that they could have a brief, blazing affair. But brief affairs, blazing or otherwise, were not her style, as she'd tried to tell him before he'd left. She couldn't imagine anything more developing between them.

Was it her lack of encouragement that seemed to make him even more determined to pursue her? Was that such a rarity for him that it piqued his male ego, presenting him with a challenge he couldn't resist?

Why was she spending so much time worrying about this? All she had to do was say no when he called to ask her out. Or send him away if he showed up on her doorstep again. She had, on occasion, dealt with unwanted male attentions before. Maybe what worried her most was that Perry's attentions weren't entirely unwanted.

"Or maybe," she said out loud again, "you're just using Perry as a diversion to keep you from writing."

"Who are you talking to, Kristin?"

Kristin jumped so violently that her pad fell from her lap. "Mother, you nearly gave me a heart attack," she scolded, one hand on her pounding chest. "I didn't hear you arrive."

Wearing a colorful, flowing ensemble that made her resemble a walking rainbow, Sophie strolled to a chair near Kristin's and nodded toward the tea pitcher. "That looks good."

Kristin leaned forward to nudge her glass toward her mother. "Take this one. I haven't touched it yet. I'll get another glass for myself."

It took her only a few moments to go into the kitchen for another glass. She used that brief time to compose herself and prepare for a session of maternal grilling. When she returned to the deck, she found her mother sipping her tea and studying the blank pages of Kristin's writing pad.

"Apparently, I arrived just as you were getting started," she commented, tossing the pad on the table. "I'm sorry, dear. I hope I didn't break your train of thought."

"Don't worry. That train derailed long before you got here," Kristin said, taking her seat and trying to look unconcerned.

Sophie lifted an eyebrow. "The writing's not going well?"

"No, not today. I'm sort of stuck."

Sophie smiled. "I've heard that before. Somewhere around the middle of every book, I think."

Kristin laughed lightly. "You know me, Mom. Gotta follow the same ol' routines."

Sophie's smile faded as she studied her daughter's face. "I *do* know you. What's wrong, Kristin?"

Kristin shrugged and made a production of pouring her tea. "Oh, I just have the blues, I guess. What brings you here today, Mom? I wasn't expecting you."

"I know. I just had an urge to see my little girl today."

Something in her mother's voice made Kristin look back up with narrowed eyes. "What's going on?"

Sophie had never quite mastered an innocent expression. "Why, nothing. Why do you ask?"

"Because I know *you*. There's a reason you decided to drop by today. What is it?"

Sophie sighed and shook her head. "Actually, there is something I want to discuss with you, but it really isn't a big deal."

Which meant, of course, that it *was* a big deal. "What is it?"

"Jack asked me to go to Australia with him. He's leaving in a few days."

Kristin felt her jaw drop. "*Australia?*"

Sophie nodded, her cheeks suspiciously pink. "He's going for a three-week visit to several areas of interest there. It sounds like a fascinating vacation."

"And you're going with him?"

"I think so. You know how I've always wanted to see Australia. It's been a lifelong dream of mine, but I wasn't sure I'd ever have the chance."

Kristin shook her head slowly. "I know you've always wanted to go there, but are you sure you want to go with Jack? You're talking about a vacation that will last longer than you've actually known the guy."

"I'm aware of that. But I like Jack very much. We've had a great time together. And I don't want to miss out on this wonderful opportunity."

Kristin was accustomed to her mother's impulsiveness, but this was a bit different than usual. This time Sophie was talking about going halfway around the world for nearly a month with a man she hardly knew. "I don't know, Mom. This doesn't sound like such a good idea to me."

Sophie's left eyebrow rose. "Did I give you the impression I was asking for your permission?"

"I know you don't need my permission. I thought you were asking for my advice."

"Not even that. I just wanted to let you know my plans."

"So you're definitely going."

"I've already told him yes. I'm very excited about it, Kristin."

"Then I hope you have a wonderful time," Kristin replied, knowing she had no other option. Her mother was an adult, after all. And she *had* always talked of visiting Australia someday. Kristin had no right to stand in her way just because she was worried about her.

Or was her hesitation due entirely to worry? She couldn't help wondering if part of her reservation came from sheer jealousy. Her mother was leaving for an exotic adventure with a dashing man, while Kristin would be staying behind with a looming deadline and a fear of getting involved with the only man who had interested her in a long time.

Sophie deftly changed the subject. "Have you heard from Perry since he visited you?"

"No, he hasn't called. But I didn't really expect him to."

"He said he would call, didn't he?"

"Yes, but you know how it goes. People say that sort of thing all the time."

Sophie shook her head. "If Perry said he would call, he'll call."

"And how would you know that? You've never even met Perry."

"I've seen him many times on TV. He has honest

eyes. And I'm sure he's smart enough to know what a catch you are."

Kristin rolled her eyes. "I am not a fish."

Laughing, Sophie refilled her glass. "No, but you're a catch, anyway. Tell me more about him."

"There's really not much more I can tell you about him than what you've gotten out of me over the phone. I really don't know Perry all that well, and I don't expect to see him again soon, if ever. I told him I'm very busy with my work right now."

"Darling, you may be busy, but you aren't dead. You can't just lock yourself up in this house. It's no wonder you're having trouble writing. You have to experience life to write about it."

"I'm hardly a hermit, Mom. In fact, I've been so busy 'experiencing life' lately, I've hardly had time to write."

Sophie didn't buy that excuse. "You've taken one week off in the past four or five months. You've only been on one date since you got back from New York and that was only because Perry gave you little choice. You're too young to lead such a quiet existence, sweetie. You need to live a little."

Kristin had heard this speech so many times her response was automatic. "I'm doing fine, Mom."

"That's what you always say. But it doesn't explain why you looked so worried when I got here. And it doesn't explain why you have no time for a handsome, charming, exciting single man."

"So, when are you leaving for Australia?" At that moment, Kristin was almost tempted to help her mother pack.

Fortunately, Sophie was excited enough about

her upcoming trip that she fell for the obvious ruse to change the subject.

PERRY REALLY KNEW BETTER than to keep showing up at Kristin's door without calling first. Contrary to the evidence, his mother had raised him with better manners than that. But every time he'd picked up the phone to call her, he'd set it back down. He hadn't wanted to hear her voice with too many miles between them. He hadn't wanted to give her the chance to tell him she didn't want to see him again.

He wasn't sure if his uninvited appearance at her door was an act of cowardice or bravery.

It wasn't Kristin who answered when he rang the doorbell. Perry blinked at the colorful sight that greeted him. The woman had flame-red hair and was draped in flowing, brightly hued clothing. Though her dark brown eyes were her only resemblance to Kristin, Perry recognized her, anyway, from the photograph on Kristin's mantel. "You're Kristin's mother."

"Sophie Cole," she said, giving him a bright smile. "And you're Perry Goodman. What a pleasure it is to meet you."

He took her extended hand, liking her at first sight. "The pleasure is all mine, Mrs. Cole. How was your parachute jump?"

She laughed musically. "It was a blast. Please, come in, Mr. Goodman. Can I get you something to drink?"

"No, thank you. And please, call me Perry." He closed the door behind them, noting that Kristin wasn't in sight.

Settling gracefully onto one end of the couch, Sophie waved him to a chair. "Kristin left just before you got here to pick up some things for dinner. She should be back in twenty minutes or so."

"She wasn't expecting me. I'm afraid I've shown up without warning."

"Good move." Sophie nodded firmly. "If you'd called, she'd have found an excuse to keep you away."

"That's pretty much what I was thinking." Because she seemed to be on his side, he asked frankly, "Why is that, do you suppose? Is it something I've done?"

"Oh, don't take it personally. Kristin hasn't dated *anyone* lately. I've spent all afternoon fussing at her about that...not that it does any good."

Perry thought of the photograph that had been bugging him for the past couple of days—the one in which Kristin had looked so intimate with the man at the amusement park. "Is it because of the man she was dating before? The big sandy-haired guy?"

"Jim Hooper? She told you about him?" Sophie seemed surprised.

"I accidentally saw a snapshot. She said you took it at an amusement park last year."

Sophie's carefully penciled eyebrows drew into a frown. "We had taken Jim's daughter Kimberly to the park for her birthday. Jim and Kristin broke up a week after those photographs were taken."

Perry tried to think of a relatively tactful way to ask a question that was absolutely none of his business.

Sophie didn't give him a chance to ask. "He

went back to his wife, the jerk. After he spent months assuring Kristin that his marriage was completely over and that he had no feelings left for his wife, it turned out he'd been courting his ex again the whole time. He was just using my daughter to keep him company and stroke his ego until he could convince his wife to take him back."

Perry winced. "Was Kristin badly hurt?"

"Her pride was damaged. She hated knowing she'd been so completely fooled. But mostly she was upset because she had grown so fond of Kimberly. After Jim broke up with her, Kristin never saw that little girl again."

Sophie sighed and shook her head. "She wouldn't appreciate me telling you this, of course. And I won't tell you any more. I just thought you should know what you're up against."

"Thank you."

Her sudden bright smile reminded him forcibly of Kristin. Sophie even had that same little wrinkle across her nose—which made Perry like her even more. "I've had hopes for you ever since Kristin bought you at that auction," she confided. "From what little she's told me about you, I know she likes you...but she's understandably worried about getting hurt again. My daughter is a strong, competent woman—but she has some insecurities. Sometimes I blame them on myself," she admitted.

"Er..." Perry didn't quite know what to say. Sophie was a talker—and not a particularly discreet one, at that. He imagined she would be a hard act to follow for a daughter who tended to be a bit more on the quiet side.

"Her father died when she was very young, and

I'm not sure I was the most stabilizing influence during her youth. I love her dearly, of course, and I've always tried to be there for her...but there are people who have labeled me as...well, flighty."

Since she looked more rueful than distressed, Perry smiled. "I don't know Kristin very well yet, but I do know she adores her mother."

Sophie smiled sweetly. "Yes, she does. I'm just saying that she and I are rather different, no matter how much we care for each other. I thought I'd try to explain her a little so you'll know her better."

"I think that's for me to find out for myself, don't you?" he asked carefully.

She nodded, then immediately continued. "She also seems to be concerned about her writing lately. She won't talk to me about it, but I don't think it's going very well."

"She mentioned the same thing to me."

"Have you read any of her books, Perry?"

He cleared his throat. "No, I haven't had a chance to read one yet."

"My daughter is a very talented writer. Her books are fresh and witty and spicy, and she has many devoted fans who find great pleasure in her stories. The books celebrate love and family and romance—and I think maybe that's part of her problem. She's having trouble writing about romance, because after all Jim's lies, she's having trouble believing in it, at least for herself."

Perry wondered if she was giving him advice on how to court her daughter. Romance? He'd never considered himself an expert in the art, though he'd had his share of relationships. And was Sophie advocating that he pursue an affair with her daughter—a rather unlikely possibility—or was she beginning to hear imaginary wedding bells?

As fascinated as Perry had become with Kristin Cole, and as determined as he was to spend more time with her, he was a long way from being ready to think about that sort of commitment. He'd dated Jennifer nearly two years before he'd asked her to marry him, and look what a mistake that carefully thought-out decision had turned out to be. But maybe he was making too much of Sophie's encouragement. Maybe she just wanted her daughter to relax and have a good time—something Perry was entirely willing to offer.

"Do you have any more advice for me, Sophie?"

She laughed. "No, I'm afraid you're on your own now. I've just given you a little insight about Kristin that I thought would be helpful to you. And I'm trusting you to use that knowledge wisely. Hurt my baby, and I'll make your political enemies seem like your best friends."

"You sound very fierce, Mrs. Cole."

Her smile showed teeth. "I intended to, Mr. Goodman. If you are only toying with my daughter, you can leave now and she'll never know you were here."

Perry settled more comfortably into his chair, his fingers steepled in front of him. "I didn't rearrange half a dozen appointments, fly to Raleigh, rent a car and drive all the way here just to leave without even seeing her."

She nodded in satisfaction. "I don't imagine you'd go to all that trouble if all you're interested in is a mere one-night stand."

"What I'm interested in," he informed her gently, "is between me and your daughter."

Rather than taking offense, Sophie laughed in apparent delight. "I like you very much, Perry Goodman."

He grinned back at her. "I like you, too, Sophie Cole."

"Well, then." She rose, scooping a red leather purse off the coffee table. "I'll be on my way now. Be good to my daughter, Perry—or maybe I should say be good *for* her."

Perry stood quickly. "Are you going?"

"Yes. You kids don't need Mama hanging around this evening. If I'm here, Kristin will just sit back and let me do all the talking—and trust me, I would." She extended her right hand. "I can expect to see you again, Mr. Goodman?"

Because it seemed appropriate with this woman, Perry lifted her hand to his lips. "Count on it, Mrs. Cole."

7

KRISTIN COULD HARDLY SEE over the bags in her arms as she struggled to the front door. She probably should have made two trips, but she was still annoyed and impatient because of a delay at the supermarket. Balancing one bulky bag on her knee, she managed to get the door open.

"Mom? Can you grab one of these bags? I'm about to—"

Strong arms lifted all the bags from hers. "These are too heavy. You should have made more than one trip."

Kristin stared at the man who was gently scolding her even as he easily balanced the two heavy bags. Was she hallucinating? No. The way her pulse suddenly tripped into double-time let her know he was really standing there, close enough for her to reach out and touch him.

She curled her fingers to keep herself from doing just that. "Perry? What are you...?"

"Where do you want these?" he asked as if he couldn't imagine why she'd be surprised to find him in her house. "Kitchen?"

"Yes." She looked around in vain for Sophie. "Where's my mother?"

"She said to tell you she had a sudden urge to

visit your aunt Myrtle," he said over his shoulder.

"Do you really have an aunt Myrtle?"

Kristin followed him to the kitchen, trying to understand what had happened in the short time she'd been gone. "Yes, of course, Mother's sister. When did Mother leave?"

"Twenty minutes ago." He set the bags on the counter and began to dig into them. "I've been waiting for you since then. I was starting to get worried. She told me you should be back any minute after she left."

"I got behind a cretin at the grocery store. Perry, what are you doing here? And why did Mother leave? She was going to stay for dinner. Did you say something to her?"

"I asked her to stay. I would have enjoyed visiting with her longer. She was delightful. But she wouldn't stay. She seemed to have the idea that you and I might want to be alone together."

"What did she say to *you*?" Knowing her mother so well, Kristin was much more concerned about that.

Perry practically buried his head in the bag he was unpacking. "Nothing much. What are we having? Pasta?"

"I was planning to make pasta for my mother."

"It would be a shame to let all this food go to waste. What can I do to help you make dinner? Remember, you told me last time I visited that you'd teach me to cook?"

Kristin shook off her initial disorientation and frowned at him. "Why do you keep showing up without calling first? Haven't you ever heard of the telephone?"

He met her look blandly. "You never gave me your number."

"I'm listed, Goodman. You found my address, I'm sure you could have found my number if you'd tried."

"Maybe." He looked at the groceries scattered on the counter around him. "What do we do first?"

She didn't quite know how it had happened, but it looked as though Kristin would be spending the evening giving Perry a cooking lesson. She debated silently for a moment over whether she should request that he leave—but even as the thought crossed her mind, she knew she would not. He looked undeniably appealing in her kitchen, dressed in khakis and a forest green pullover, a package of pasta in one hand and a bunch of fresh spinach in the other.

She sighed. "You can start chopping vegetables."

"Great," he said cheerily. "Where do you keep your knives?"

She blinked in response to his enthusiasm. "Er...maybe you should boil water and I'll chop vegetables."

He laughed. "I can be trusted with a knife. Just get me started."

Kristin was determined to get through this evening politely, but without enjoying it too much. After all, she hadn't invited Perry to her house for dinner. She'd even told him straight out that she didn't have time to entertain him at present, with her deadline looming so close. But he'd totally ignored her hints and shown up, anyway, as if her concerns weren't to be taken seriously. She wouldn't be rude enough to ask him to leave—this time—but she didn't have to have fun.

Perry, of course, had other ideas.

She should have expected that a man who made his living being charming and personable would be hard to resist when it gave it his full effort. She couldn't help laughing at his jokes and being amused by his efforts to understand the recipe she handed him. He hinted at the beginning of the impromptu cooking lesson that a glass of wine would be nice. By the time they'd both had a couple of glasses, she was having a much harder time keeping her emotional distance.

Perry slid the casserole dish into the oven and rubbed his hands together. "How long does it bake?"

"Half an hour. The salad's in the refrigerator, and I bought hard rolls to go with it, so there's really nothing left to do until the timer beeps."

Perry set his wineglass on the counter and took a step toward her. "I'm sure we can think of something to do to fill the time."

She moved quickly backward. "Why don't we take a walk outside?"

His smile was rueful. "Yeah, sure. That's something like what I had in mind."

Checking her watch so she'd be sure to gauge the cooking time correctly, Kristin opened the back door and led Perry outside. Taking a leisurely walk down to the water would be much safer than staying inside with him when he had that wicked gleam in his eyes.

It was a very pleasant evening. The sky had turned a lovely shade of lavender and a cool breeze rustled leaves above their heads. "It's nice out here," Perry commented, stopping to admire a small rose garden she had planted around a concrete fountain. "I see several bird feeders. Are you a bird-watcher?"

"I love to sit on my deck in the mornings and watch the birds. I get a lot of different types here."

"It's been a while since I've had a free morning to watch the wildlife." He sounded a bit envious. "Do you ever see deer from those woods?"

"Yes, they wander into my yard quite often. In the winter I put corn out for them."

They had reached the back boundary of her property. Kristin led him to the path through the woods that would take them down to the water's edge. She heard Perry make a sound of appreciation when they stepped out of the trees and onto the rocky shoreline of the private, manmade lake. Several homes, some with their own docks, were visible from where they stood. They could see a couple of fishing boats out on the water, little more than toy-size dots in the distance. Like the sky, the water had taken on a purply-blue hue, with ripples of waves kicked up by the brisk breeze.

"This is great," Perry murmured. "I bet you spend a lot of time here."

She led him to a large, flat-topped boulder in the shade of a large tree. The rock was just large enough for both of them to sit down. "I sit here a lot and watch the water lap against the shore. The fish jump and the birds skim the water looking for dinner. Sometimes the deer even come out to drink."

Sitting beside her, Perry spread his long legs in front of him. "Do you ever fish?"

"No. I'm content just to sit and enjoy."

He scooped a small flat pebble from the ground at his feet. With a deft flick of his wrist, he sent it skipping across the surface of the water. "Haven't done that since I was a kid."

"You're still very good at it," she assured him gravely. "It must have skipped six or seven times."

"Ten."

She lifted an eyebrow. "Ten? You think so?"

"I know so. I counted."

"Mmm."

"You doubt me?"

"Let's just say I know you politicians like to put a positive spin on things."

He leaned forward to search the ground, then picked up another small, flat rock. "Count," he said, and sent the rock flying across the water.

It sank on the tenth skip. "Okay," Kristin conceded. "We'll count that as ten."

Perry nodded in satisfaction. "I've told you, I'm not the kind of politician you seem to think I am."

She cleared her throat and glanced at her watch, having no intention of getting into a political discussion with him. "We'd better head back to the house. By the time we wash up, our dinner will be ready."

He stood and extended his hand to her. She placed hers in it, letting him draw her to her feet. He didn't immediately release her. Instead, he pulled her toward him. "I can't think of a more perfect place to steal a kiss," he murmured, and proceeded to do so.

It really was a lovely place for a surprise kiss, Kristin thought, clutching his shirt. The only thing marring her pleasure in the moment was her certainty that she would never again come to this spot without remembering it...and him.

Perry drew back before the embrace escalated. "I was right," he said. "It was perfect."

She moistened her lips and almost shivered when she tasted him there. "We, uh, we'd better go check on our dinner."

PERRY SEEMED ALMOST surprised when he took a bite of the spinach lasagna they'd prepared together. "Hey, this is really good!"

Kristin couldn't help laughing. "You were expecting it to be bad?"

He swallowed a second bite. "Delicious. Cooking's not really all that hard, is it?"

"No, not if you start with relatively simple dishes and carefully follow directions."

"Do you mind if I take a copy of the recipe with me? I'd like to try making it again."

Kristin couldn't help wondering who he wanted to impress with his novice culinary skills. She looked down at her meal as she replied, "You're welcome to the recipe, of course."

He ate in silent appreciation for a few moments, then asked, "How's your book coming?"

She promptly lost her appetite. "Slowly."

"You said it wasn't going well. What's the problem?"

She shrugged. "It's hard to explain."

"I've been told I'm a good listener."

She didn't doubt that. The problem was she

didn't know how to make him understand what she didn't understand herself. Why she, who had written a dozen books and enjoyed nearly every minute of doing so, was suddenly finding herself struggling to finish a page. Dreading the next time she sat at the computer. Devoid of any fresh ideas, when ideas had once been so plentiful in her head that she had hardly been able to contain them. "There's really nothing to say."

"I've met a few writers. It isn't an easy job, is it?"

"Some people think it's very easy. All you have to do is make up a story."

"Who was it that said all you have to do is sit at the typewriter and open a vein?"

She smiled, recognizing the allusion. "Hemingway, I think."

"Does it feel that way for you?"

"I never thought of it as so painful...until recently."

"What's gone wrong?"

"I don't know," she murmured, wishing he would just drop the subject. "I'm just in a temporary slump, I guess. And it doesn't help," she added a bit peevishly, "that people keep dropping in on me without notice."

"I can see where that would become annoying," he commiserated. "You should probably tell them to stop."

"I've tried. Some people just don't take hints."

He clicked his tongue. "Ain't it the truth. Want me to refill your wineglass?"

She nodded absently. "So what have *you* been up to the past few days?" she asked, mostly to change the subject.

"Meetings. Luncheons. Dinners. The usual."

"I saw your picture in a newsmagazine. You were talking to Senator Reynolds."

He nodded. "I saw that one. The tag line implied that he and I were discussing an important campaign strategy."

"And were you?"

He grinned. "He was telling me about his daughter's new boyfriend. The guy has a ponytail, a safety pin through his tongue and a tattoo that reads Have a Knife Day. He was asking if I thought it would hurt his chances for reelection if he took the kid out for a hike in the woods and 'accidentally' lost him."

"Senator Reynolds's daughter is dating a boy like that?" Kristin didn't try to hide her amazement. "No wonder he's upset. He always comes across as stepping straight out of the 1950s."

Perry's smile dimmed a bit. "Larry's a genuinely nice guy. Most of the garbage you've read to the contrary has been manufactured by his liberal opposition."

"And how much garbage have you 'manufactured' against his liberal opposition?"

"I have never distributed any information that I didn't believe to be true. I'll admit I've been duped a couple of times into defending candidates who didn't deserve my misguided loyalty, but that was when I was younger, less experienced and more willing to believe what I wanted to hear."

"So all your candidates now are fine, honest, upstanding citizens who only have the country's best interest at heart and have no hidden agendas of their own?" She made no effort to hide her skepticism.

"All the candidates I work for have convinced me they are the best men and women for the offices they are seeking," he answered firmly. "They're human, they make mistakes and have a few flaws, but I believe in them or I wouldn't be supporting them."

Kristin couldn't help thinking there were times when Perry Goodman sounded just too good to be true. *Like Jim,* a nagging little voice inside her whispered. She sipped her wine, then set the glass on the table. "I think you should know that I rarely vote for your party. Old-fashioned conservatives tend to make me nervous."

He shrugged. "Some of them scare the hell out of me. So do some of the off-the-wall liberals. My personal candidates tend to be more in the middle. Just a little right of center, for the most part."

"And I guess you'd consider me a little left of center."

He grinned, showing no concern. "Should make for some interesting after-dinner debates."

She frowned and shook her head. "I *never* debate politics, religion or the definition of a 'good' book. Some people—my mother, for one—love to get into noisy, heated arguments. I prefer quiet, courteous conversations."

"So do I, for the most part. And for the record, I would never belittle your political beliefs. I would assume you've given them serious consideration and have very good reasons for forming your opinions. I respect that even when my own choices are different."

Kristin bit her lip, aware that her usual decision-making process when it came to politics was sort of close-her-eyes-and-pick-one. She had just never been particularly interested in the entire process. Perry was giving her too much credit, which wasn't the way she had expected him to react to her announcement that she didn't support his party.

She reached again for her wineglass. Perry Goodman was proving more difficult to discourage than she had predicted, though she still wasn't sure exactly what he wanted from her. He was almost impossible to read. She only hoped he didn't turn out to be equally impossible to resist.

SOMETIME BETWEEN THE MAIN course and the strawberry cake Kristin served for dessert, Perry reached a decision. She had been badly hurt by a man she had trusted, leaving her wary of trusting so easily again. She was anxious and stressed-out about her work, and her tension was probably contributing to the difficulty she'd been having. She needed to relax and she needed to learn to trust again. Until then, he didn't have a chance with her.

Which meant, he thought regretfully, he had to call on every ounce of patience he possessed—never his strong suit—to allow her to find out for herself that he was a man she could count on.

He didn't stay long after helping her clear away the dishes. He really didn't want to leave, but it seemed the best course of action. Kristin walked him to the door, her expression giving no indication of how she felt about his early departure.

"I had a very nice evening," he told her at the door. "Thank you for the cooking lesson."

"I had a good time, too," she admitted. "But, Perry, call first next time, will you?"

He nodded quickly, before she could realize she had just implicitly committed to a next time.

He reached out to cup her face between his hands. "You'll be hearing from me soon. I'm having too much trouble staying away from you."

She reached up as if by reflex to touch his hands with hers. "I enjoy visiting with you, Perry. But there's little else I can offer for now."

"Then that will have to be enough—for now." He brushed his lips across her forehead and then the tip of her incredibly cute nose. And then he touched his lips to hers, exerting massive self-control to keep the kiss light and relatively chaste when he wanted so much more.

He drew back slowly, smiling faintly down at her. "Someday..." he murmured, then let the sentence trail away unfinished. Taking a deep breath to bolster his willpower, he released her and stepped away. "Good night, Kristin. Sleep well."

He left quickly—before he gave in to the almost overwhelming urge to take her in his arms and carry her off to bed.

THE PACKAGE ARRIVED LATE the next morning. Kristin might have expected flowers—and probably wouldn't have been overly touched by them, since flowers were such a standard gesture.

Perry sent her a magic wand.

She lifted the whimsical gift out of the package with a bemused smile. The shaft of the wand was clear plastic, filled with glitter suspended in water. A sparkling sequin-covered plastic star made up the head of the wand, and long, shiny, multicolored streamers tumbled from the bottom.

Wave this over your computer, was scrawled on the enclosed card. *It couldn't hurt.* It was signed simply, *Perry.*

He really should have just sent flowers, Kristin thought, turning the wand in her hand to allow the glitter to catch the light. She doubted that flowers would have brought such a massive lump to her throat.

She set the wand beside her computer while she worked that afternoon. She refused to accept that it made the least bit of difference, of course, but she did manage to write five pretty good pages that day. Not nearly as many pages as she needed to get even close to being back on schedule—but it was three more pages than she'd managed to write the last time she'd spent a day at the computer.

Another package arrived the next day. Kristin dug through layers of protective bubble-wrap and pulled out a six-inch-high porcelain figurine. It depicted a delicate, winged fairy clothed in a sheer floating dress, her blond hair a tousled halo around her sweet face. The fairy stood on tiptoes, leaning slightly forward, a tiny wand in her right hand. The enclosed card read only *Make A Wish.*

Perry really was going to have to stop this, she thought, setting the little figurine on her desk. It made her smile every time she looked at it that afternoon. She wrote six pages, and was satisfied with all but one of them—and that one, she decided, was fixable.

The next day's delivery came from a local florist, but rather than a bouquet of flowers, Perry had sent her a potted shamrock plant. *I've heard these are lucky*, the unsigned card read.

The plant found a home on her office windowsill.

Perry called that evening. "How's it going?" he asked without identifying himself.

"You have to stop sending me gifts," she scolded mildly.

He chuckled. "I was trying to bring you luck with your writing. Is it working?"

Since she'd written more in the past three days than she had in the preceding three weeks, she didn't quite know how to answer him. Her writing had nothing to do with his gifts, of course. She'd simply had a pretty good week. She still had a long way to go before the book was finished.

He didn't wait for her to come up with an answer. "I've missed you, Kristin."

If she had been stumped for a response before, she was doubly so now. "Um…"

"I have to fly to Dallas tomorrow for a major fund-raiser. I don't suppose you'd be free to go with me?"

"I really can't," she said, not sure if she was relieved or just slightly disappointed that she had a legitimate excuse. "I have to work."

"I was afraid of that." He sounded resigned. "We could have had fun."

She didn't doubt that, actually. She'd had fun, despite herself, whenever she was with Perry. But she really couldn't run off to Dallas with him tomorrow—for many reasons, not the least of which was her work.

"Is your writing going more smoothly?" he asked.

"Maybe a little better," she said guardedly.

"That's good news, isn't it?"

"Of course."

"You sound like you're afraid to talk about it. Superstitious?"

"No, not really. Just…cautious."

"No problem. You're sure you won't go to Dallas with me?"

She smiled, thinking he deserved some credit for persistence. "I'm sure."

"Okay. Then I'll see you when I get back. In the meantime—think of me occasionally, okay?"

As if she could help it, especially when he kept sending whimsical little gifts to remind her of him. "Have a safe trip, Perry."

"Thanks. I'll do that. Bye."

Kristin's hand was still on the receiver when the phone rang again. It was her mother, calling to chatter enthusiastically about her rapidly approaching trip.

"It's going to be so much fun," Sophie enthused. "But I wish…"

"What?" Kristin wondered if her mother was having second thoughts about taking off for Australia with a man she'd bought at an auction.

She should have known better. Sophie's only worries, as usual, were for her daughter. "I wish you were going to be having a good time, too. I feel as though I'm leaving when you need me most."

"Don't worry about me. I'm fine. You have a wonderful time."

"Maybe Perry will come see you again while I'm gone," her mother suggested hopefully. "You couldn't help but have a good time with him."

Kristin kept her mouth firmly. If Sophie found out that Kristin had just declined the chance to accompany Perry to Dallas, she would be appalled. She would do everything she could to change her daughter's mind. And because Kristin wasn't at all sure how firm her resolution was on that particular subject, anyway, she didn't need to cloud the issue with her mother's nagging.

As Kristin concluded the call a few minutes later, she reassured herself that she really couldn't have given Perry any other answer. Even if she was the type to travel with a man she hardly knew, Kristin had to work. Sophie lived on her late husband's benefits and her own retirement from thirty years of teaching public school, supplementing her income by occasionally substitute teaching. She was free to take off on spontaneous vacations whenever she wanted, unlike Kristin, who had to meet her deadlines if her bills were to be paid.

Kristin sighed and ran a hand through her hair, looking around her cluttered office. It was time to get back to work. There was nothing to disturb her now—the house was quiet and empty. Maybe a little *too* quiet and empty, she thought wistfully. Maybe she should get a cat or something.

SHE GOT A RABBIT. The plush toy arrived the next day, her delivery from Perry. It was brown-and-white with a pink nose and a shiny pink ribbon around its neck. Kristin laughed when she read the card.

If one rabbit's foot is lucky, four should be even better.

She couldn't resist lifting the impossibly soft toy to her cheek. Why couldn't the man just send flowers?

The gifts she received during the following days continued to carry the "good luck" theme. He sent a crystal box filled with pennies. *One of these must be a lucky penny*, the card assured her. The next day's delivery brought a little leprechaun doll holding a tiny pot of "gold." *Someone to keep you company*, the accompanying card informed her. The grinning little face made Kristin smile as she sat the doll on the desk beside her computer monitor.

She couldn't help wondering how much influence Perry's string of quirky gifts had to do with the sudden surge of creativity she experienced during the next week. She found herself getting deeper and deeper into her story. Her characters came to life, moving through the pages with more spirit and energy than she'd been able to give them a few weeks earlier.

Nick O'Donnell was quickly becoming the strongest hero she'd ever written—and Kristin didn't even try to tell herself that was only a coincidence. She was fully, wryly aware that Nick had taken on more and more of Perry's finest traits— his charm, his spontaneity, his sense of humor, the high ideals he expressed about his job and his commitments. On paper, he was the perfect romance hero.

As for whether he would ever be *her* hero—well,

that was another question. One that made her extremely nervous even to consider at this point.

Her office was getting crowded, she thought, looking at the gifts Perry had sent her. Surely he would stop soon. But she knew she would be quite disappointed when he did.

8

PERRY SAT IN HIS WASHINGTON, D.C. office, a half-dozen files stacked in front of him, a graph of recent poll results on his computer screen and a pile of phone messages at his elbow. He had a great deal of work to do that afternoon.

Someone tapped on his office door and he looked up from the list he had been studying. "Come in."

Elspeth entered, carrying a stack of bound reports. "Perry, I need..."

"What else brings luck?" he interrupted, still lost in his own thoughts.

She paused. "What are you talking about?"

"Lucky things," he repeated. "You know, like four-leaf clovers."

She nodded in sudden comprehension. "Oh, you mean charms. Like rabbits' feet."

"Did that. What else?"

"Um—lucky pennies?"

"Did it."

"My father has a pair of lucky socks," she offered. "He wears them every time he plays golf."

Perry frowned. "Lucky socks? Whoever heard of lucky socks?"

He couldn't send socks to Kristin. Not only were

they completely unromantic, she'd never understand the purpose.

"What exactly do you need this for, anyway?" Elspeth asked curiously. "Do we have a superstitious candidate I don't know about?"

"No, uh…" Aware that he'd been spending a bit too much time on his "lucky list" when he had so much else to do, Perry cleared his throat and rubbed the back of his neck. "It's a, um, personal project," he said, setting the list aside.

Elspeth studied him intently. "Does it have something to do with Kristin Cole?"

He cleared his throat and avoided her eyes. "Maybe. What of it?"

He heard the amusement in her voice when she replied, "Oh, nothing. Just curious."

He rolled his pen between his fingers. For some reason, he felt compelled to say something more. "She's been having some problems with her writing. I've sent her a couple of things to cheer her up."

"Mmm. I've heard about some of the rather interesting packages that have gone out of here lately."

He scowled. "Who's been talking about my personal business?"

"Everyone," she answered cheerfully.

"Oh, great." He tossed his pen down in disgust. A guy couldn't even get to know a fascinating woman around here without everyone whispering about it behind his back.

Elspeth laughed. "Can you blame us? You've hardly been acting like yourself lately. You're distracted, kind of moody. You keep trying to arrange time off—which you have to admit is unusual for you. *And* you were spotted holding a romance novel yesterday during Senator Buckle's speech."

He felt his cheeks grow warm. "Mary Alice brought me a couple of Kristin's books. I want to read them, but I haven't been able to find the time yet."

"You really like her, don't you, Perry?"

"Of course I like her," he answered lightly, picking up his pen again.

Elspeth shook her head. "It's more than that. You're besotted. Big time."

"I don't know that I'd put it that way," he protested, uncomfortable with her phrasing.

"I would. If you'd devoted this much time to Jennifer, you'd be a married man now."

Perry grimaced automatically. He didn't even want to think about that scenario. Though he'd once considered Jennifer the perfect political and social mate, he couldn't even imagine himself married to her now.

He refused to picture himself married to anyone else in particular.

"What can I do for you, Elspeth?" he asked, deliberately changing the subject.

She hesitated only a moment before following his lead. For the next fifteen minutes, they talked business. Elspeth paused on her way out when the conversation was concluded. "A horseshoe," she said.

"A what?"

"A horseshoe. They're lucky."

"Oh. Yeah, I'd forgotten about that one. Thanks."

She smiled. "Anything for such a good cause."

Perry stared at his door for several minutes after Elspeth closed it behind her. He had managed to keep his mind on business for a few minutes, but now his thoughts were filled with Kristin again.

Even as he scribbled the word *horseshoe* on his list, he heard the echo of Elspeth's unsettling comment. *If you'd devoted this much time to Jennifer, you'd be a married man now.*

KRISTIN SAW THE PHOTOGRAPH of Perry only an hour or so after her daily package from him arrived.

This time he'd sent a brass oil lamp, like the one in the Aladdin story. *Maybe it doesn't hold a genie, but it's guaranteed to brighten a dark day*, Perry had written on the card.

Kristin realized she hadn't had many dark days since she'd met Perry. His visits had entertained her, and the whimsical gifts he'd sent had given her something to look forward to when he was away.

She wished he would call, she thought, looking a bit longingly at the telephone. She missed him.

That thought sobered her. Her smile fading, she set the lamp on a shelf and turned away from it. She was trying so hard not to start weaving unlikely daydreams around Perry Goodman. She wanted to be realistic in her expectations.

Sure, he was paying a lot of very flattering attention to her now. She was a novelty to him. A woman who hadn't fallen at his feet in gratitude that he'd even noticed her.

Or was she being unfair? she couldn't help wondering a bit guiltily. Perry had given her no reason to think he was that arrogant. Could it be that she'd formed an opinion about him without really getting to know him? She hated it when people stereotyped romance writers; but maybe she'd been guilty of doing the same to people who made their living in the political arena.

And then she saw his photograph in the newsmagazine that had arrived in that day's mail.

He'd been captured at a fund-raising event in Texas, a barbecue hosted by the governor. On his arm was a tall, beautiful blonde Kristin recognized. The small print beneath the snapshot identified them as "Perry Goodman And His Associate And Frequent Companion, Elspeth Moore."

Elspeth was his friend, Kristin reminded herself. His co-worker. She'd been very pleasant to Kristin on the night of her first date with Perry.

Frequent companion. Just how much time did Perry spend with Elspeth? And how could he be with her and not notice that she was drop-dead gorgeous in addition to being intelligent and charming?

Kristin closed the magazine. She didn't like the way seeing that photograph had made her feel. The sensation was uncomfortably close to jealousy—and that was an emotion she had dealt with far too painfully in her last relationship.

She set the magazine aside, telling herself to put the photo—and the past—out of her mind and get back to work. She needed to make some notes for the next chapter. She pulled a legal pad out in front of her and picked up a pen. She'd written only a couple of words when the pen ran out of ink.

Sighing in frustration, she tossed the disposable pen aside and searched her desk for another. Not finding one immediately, she opened a drawer of her desk and rummaged around in it for a new package of pens.

She was going to have to clean out her desk, she thought irritably. It was a mess. Stuffed with un-filed contracts and correspondence and...

She went suddenly still, looking down at the sheet of paper she'd pulled out of the drawer. It was a child's drawing, rendered in brightly colored crayon, depicting three awkwardly proportioned people holding hands and wearing huge smiles. The figures had been labeled Daddy, Kristin and Me. The "me" was Jim's eight-year-old daughter, Kimberly.

Kristin touched a finger to the funny little face in the drawing. She had once hoped to become Kim-berly's stepmother. She still didn't know for cer-tain whether she'd fallen more seriously in love with Jim or with his daughter. She had missed Jim a little when he'd dumped her so abruptly—but she had grieved for Kimberly.

She had believed every word Jim had told her. He'd sounded so sincere. He'd seemed so genu-inely smitten with her. And all the time he'd been begging his ex-wife to take him back. A request she had finally granted.

Kristin stuffed the drawing back into the drawer and closed it with a loud snap. She would work later, she thought, pushing away from her desk. For now, she needed to get out of this house— away from her memories, away from Perry's gifts, away from her fears. She needed to be with people who accepted her and made her laugh. And the best place to find that was the soda fountain downtown where the locals hung out for ice cream sundaes and idle conversation—both of which she needed badly today.

WHEN HER DOORBELL RANG the next afternoon, Kristin was certain it was another delivery from Perry. And even though she had spent twenty-four hours trying to convince herself she really should put an end to this, she was still smiling in anticipation when she opened the door. She wondered what he had sent her this time.

She was both stunned and delighted that this time he had sent himself.

"I hope that pretty smile is meant for me." Standing on her doorstep, looking better than any man had a right to in his tailored dark suit, crisp shirt, silk tie and sexy suspenders, Perry reached out to touch her cheek with his fingertips.

She felt her smile widen. She couldn't hide the surge of pleasure she felt at seeing him. "Hello, Perry."

"It's good to see you again, Kristin."

Shaking off her surprise, she tried to sound stern when she spoke again. "I thought you were going to call first this time."

"Sorry. I forgot." He tried to look repentant but didn't pull it off very well. He held out his left hand, offering her a small, wrapped package that just fit his palm. "I brought you something."

"Another gift? Really, Perry, you have to stop this."

He smiled ruefully. "I know. I'm running out of ideas."

That wasn't what she'd meant and he knew it. She looked at the package in his hand another moment, then stepped back, resisting the impulse to grab it. "Come in."

He moved past her, then waited until she closed the door before pressing the package into her hands. "Consider this a souvenir from Texas."

Since there seemed to be nothing else she could do, she took the gift and nodded toward a chair. "Have a seat," she offered, even as she settled onto the couch.

Rather than taking one of the chairs, Perry sat beside her on the couch. "How have you been?"

"Fine, thank you." She toyed with the ribbon tied on top of the small box, but made no effort to open it. "How was Texas?"

He smiled. "Hot. But other than that, everything was fine. And your book? Is it going well?"

"I've made some progress."

His dimples flashed. "So maybe something I sent brought you luck?"

Her eyebrows rose. "Or maybe I just worked past the rough spot on my own?"

He chuckled. "That's a much more likely explanation."

Kristin sighed and wrinkled her nose. He'd gone to a lot of trouble to send her those gifts. The least she could do was act appreciative, especially since she really had enjoyed them. "But your good-luck charms didn't hurt. Thank you."

"You're welcome." He touched the unopened

package in her hands. "Aren't you curious about this one?"

She'd been stalling. She had a feeling that whatever he'd brought her this time was different from the frivolous little gifts he'd sent before. Moistening her lips, she tugged off the ribbon and peeled away the paper, knowing she couldn't delay any longer.

The box she revealed was obviously intended to hold jewelry. And that only made her all the more nervous. She swallowed hard before lifting the lid.

Inside, nestled on a bed of snowy white velvet, was a gold link bracelet. The center link was shaped like a horseshoe, encrusted with diamonds.

"I've been assured that horseshoes bring good luck," Perry said, watching her face.

She couldn't think of anything to say. The bracelet was lovely—but she wasn't at all sure she should accept it. This *was* different from the other gifts. The others had made her smile. This one made her nervous.

"You really shouldn't have done this," she said.

"I was going to bring you a real horseshoe, but the horse wouldn't cooperate. Did you know those suckers are nailed on?"

She didn't smile at his lame joke. "Perry, I can't accept this. It's too much."

"It's just another good luck charm."

She shook her head. "This is jewelry."

"And that makes it different?"

"Yes."

"Why?"

She bit her lip. "I don't know, but it does," she said after a moment.

"Kristin." She wasn't looking at him, but she heard the smile in his voice. "That isn't very logical."

"I can't help it." She wasn't able to resist touching her fingertip to the little horseshoe. It was such a pretty bauble. And then she made herself close the box. "Thank you, but you'd better take it back."

"I can't." He held up his hands so she couldn't put the box in them. "It was on sale. No returns."

"I don't believe that."

He only smiled at her.

"Then give it to one of your other lady friends," she insisted.

"Can't," he said again. "I'm not on a gift-giving basis with any of my other friends who happen to be women."

"You aren't on a gift-giving basis with *me*," she reminded him firmly.

His grin was purely wicked. "You've already accepted several gifts from me."

"But this one is different," she insisted again.

Perry laughed and reached for her. "This," he said, pulling her into his arms, "could go on all day. And I can think of much more pleasant ways to spend the time than arguing."

She opened her mouth to argue, but he didn't give her a chance. He smothered the words with his mouth.

Kristin had two choices at that point: she could do what she *should* do or what she *wanted* to do. Because she so often chose the former and so rarely the latter, she indulged herself this time. She kissed him back with all the pent-up hunger that had been building in her since she had last seen him.

Perry twisted so that his back was against the couch and Kristin was practically sitting in his lap. She didn't know what became of the bracelet, but her hands were suddenly free. She took advantage of the opportunity to run her fingers through his thick, soft hair. His hands were all over her—her back, her hips, her waist, her thigh—and she almost purred in reaction to the petting.

It had been so long since anyone had enjoyed her so thoroughly, and brought her so much pleasure in the process.

"I've missed you, Kristin," he murmured against her mouth.

She murmured a response and kissed him again, wondering if any other man had ever felt so good to her.

Somehow her shirt came unbuttoned. And somehow his hand found its way inside it, his thumb slipping beneath her bra to glide over her nipple. It hardened instantly.

His kisses changed, from hurried and eager to slow and carnal. His tongue slipped between her lips, probing deeply, thoroughly. She welcomed him inside, engaging him in a seductive thrust and parry that eventually drew a deep groan from him.

"Kristin," he muttered, cupping her face between his hands. "If you only knew how many times during the past few days I've thought about kissing you again. If you only knew what it does to me to kiss you."

Since she was sitting in his lap, she knew exactly what kissing her did to him. And she reveled in the knowledge that she could make him want her so badly. It seemed like such a long time since any man had wanted her. Since she had wanted a man in return.

She drew back a few inches to look at him. He sat very still, letting her memorize his face with her eyes and her fingertips. Very slowly, she traced the arch of his eyebrows, the straight bridge of his nose, the dimples in his cheeks, the curve of his lower lip and the faintest of clefts in his chin. He didn't feel like a stranger to her, she mused. When had he become someone she could recognize by touch alone? Why did it feel so right, so very natural to touch him? To kiss him?

Why did it suddenly seem as if this had been inevitable from the moment he'd stepped into the spotlight on that stage in New York, giving Kristin little choice, it had seemed, but to bid on him?

She knew exactly what she was doing at this moment. Exactly where this was leading. She knew if she was going to stop it, now was the time. Waiting any longer would be too cruel to both of them.

But she knew with sudden certainty that she wasn't going to stop it.

Maybe it was because she'd been so lonely. Maybe it was because her mother had flown off on an exotic vacation with a handsome man, leaving Kristin feeling dull and unadventurous in comparison. Or, more likely, it was just because this was Perry. From the moment she had first seen him, she'd known she had to have him.

Murmuring her name, he dragged a hand through her hair, gently pulling her head back to bare her throat to his lips. She shivered when he kissed the pulse in the hollow of her throat, and then used the edge of his teeth in a seductive nibble.

"Maybe we should go out for dinner or something," he muttered, lifting his head so slowly that she knew he was forcing himself to draw away.

"I just ate lunch an hour ago," she said with a tremulous smile.

He couldn't seem to resist another taste of her mouth. "Want dessert?" he asked, nibbling at her lower lip.

"I don't know." Her voice had grown huskier. "What are you offering?"

"Cake?"

She unfastened the top button of his shirt. "No."

He deftly unsnapped the front fastener of her bra. "Ice cream?"

She shivered as his warm breath brushed across her distended nipples. "No."

He covered her entire right breast with his left hand, the warmth of his palm penetrating her skin until she could feel an answering heat building inside her. "I guess we'll just have to find something else to do, instead," he murmured.

She had his shirt unbuttoned by then. Admiring the perfection she had revealed, she ran a hand slowly over his chest. The light dusting of hair tickled her skin, tempted her to brush her face against it. She'd forgotten what they'd been talking about.

She wasn't in the mood to tease any longer. She drew back far enough to look at him again. His eyes were dark, his cheeks flushed. The emotion she saw in his face wasn't feigned or calculated. He wanted her. And she found that simple fact more seductive than any of the charming little gifts he had sent her.

She rested her hand against the side of his handsome face. He caught her fingers and placed a kiss in her palm. "You are beautiful, Kristin," he murmured.

Shaking her head, she slid her hand around to cover his mouth. "Don't start giving me lines now," she ordered him. "It really isn't necessary."

She knew she wasn't beautiful. Not the way the women in Perry's world were beautiful. Jim had called her "cute." And "attractive." His ex-wife, he'd mentioned a time or two, was beautiful.

Perry pulled her hand away from his mouth, then kissed it again. "It wasn't a line. I *do* think you're beautiful. I've thought so ever since I turned and first saw you at the fund-raiser ball."

He sounded so sincere. It would be so easy to believe he meant every word he said. A politician's skill? Or was it possible that he was being honest with her? Did he really think she was...?

"Beautiful," Perry repeated, and kissed her again.

By the time they were full length on the couch, Perry stretched over her, their open shirts allowing flesh-to-flesh contact, Kristin couldn't even think coherently, much less argue. If he wanted to call her beautiful, why should she try to correct him?

She certainly found *him* beautiful—and no amount of denial on his part would have changed her mind.

He had her face cupped between his hands. She felt the fine tremors in his fingers, and she thrilled in the knowledge that she had caused them.

Against her thigh was the evidence of how very badly he wanted her—and that, too, delighted her.

Perry Goodman, she mused, was very good for her ego, even if he was a serious threat to her heart.

"Maybe we *had* better go out for dinner now," Perry said, his voice little more than a rough growl.

She smiled and shook her head, appreciating the offer even as she rejected it. "I have a better idea. Let's go to my bedroom."

His eyes glinted. "You're sure? Because if you aren't, there isn't any hurry. As much as I want to make love with you, I don't want you to have any regrets. We have plenty of time to…"

"Perry." She interrupted him with a smile, seduced all over again by the hint of uncertainty in his voice. "Thank you for your concern, but I'm a big girl. I know what I'm doing."

He didn't need any further persuasion. "In that case," he said, "show me the bedroom."

She smiled. "I thought you'd never ask."

Kristin had given serious consideration to the decoration of her bedroom. She'd spent hours selecting the perfect furnishings and accessories, fabrics and colors. If Perry noticed one detail of her decor, she would have been surprised. He never looked away from her face as they tumbled to the bed.

It was almost unnerving how intensely he focused on her. She doubted that he missed the slightest nuance of her expressions as he watched her face for reactions to the delightful things he did to her. He seemed intent on memorizing every inch of her as he slowly but efficiently stripped away her clothing. She couldn't imagine that there could be anyone else in his mind as he made love to her, murmuring her name, concentrating on pleasing her.

Within minutes he had her writhing beneath him, panting for air, aching for more. His name escaped her on a startled cry when he slipped his hand between them to take her even higher. There was certainly no other man in her mind by the time he finally gave in to her broken pleas and thrust inside her, after swiftly donning the protection she had provided from her nightstand.

She wrapped her arms and legs around him, wishing she would never have to let go, but knowing that was only a fantasy. And yet, she thought, kissing him deeply, what better time for fantasy than when Perry was in her arms?

The end was hot and fast and frantic, drawing broken cries from both of them. Before the echoes faded completely away, Perry was moving again, rolling so that she was draped on top of him. His hands on her hips guided her, giving her support until she'd regained enough strength to take over. And then she was the one in charge, making him arch and groan until he gasped in release. Only then did Kristin allow herself to climax again, giving in to the deep contractions that rocked through her. She collapsed onto Perry's chest, surprised to find that her cheeks were wet with tears of joy and pleasure.

No man had ever made her cry during lovemaking. No man had ever made love to her so thoroughly. So spectacularly. So perfectly.

Somewhere deep inside her, a worried little voice asked if any other man would ever make her feel this way again. She silenced that voice quickly, not wanting to spoil this moment.

She wanted to enjoy the fantasy just a little longer.

Perry snuggled her into his shoulder and stroked her damp hair away from her face. "Rest for now, sweetheart," he murmured. "We'll talk later."

Rest. That sounded like a wonderful idea. Kristin closed her eyes and nestled more deeply against him, soaking in his warmth like a lazy cat lying in the sun. She fell asleep with a purr of pleasure and a smile that felt distinctly feline even to her.

9

WHEN KRISTIN WOKE, she was in the bed alone. The house seemed quiet and empty. Deep shadows in the room indicated that she'd slept for at least a couple of hours. She stretched, mildly surprised when long-unused muscles protested the movement. Something felt different about her right wrist. She held it up, then laughed ruefully when she saw the gold bracelet there. The diamonds that decorated the tiny horseshoe glinted in the low light coming through the lace curtains.

Perry, she thought, was incorrigible. But, oh, was he good, she mused with a sultry smile.

She wondered where he had gone. If he was in the house, he was certainly being quiet. She reached for the short, red satin robe she had left lying on the vanity chair near the bed and tied it around her. Combing her hair with her fingers until it lay fairly smoothly around her shoulders, she left the bedroom in search of Perry.

She came to a sudden stop in the doorway to her dining room, wondering for a moment if she was still sleeping. Still dreaming.

A centerpiece of fresh-cut flowers and tall, creamy tapers sat in the middle of her table. The table was set for two with china, silver and crystal from her china cabinet. The smell of something wonderfully appetizing wafted from the kitchen.

"Perry?" she said uncertainly.

He appeared in the doorway, his hair tumbled, shirtsleeves rolled up on his forearms, a smudge of something white on the right leg of his dark slacks. "Did you have a nice nap?" he asked, as if there was nothing at all unusual about his having set her table while she slept.

"Yes...um, what are you doing?"

"I've made dinner. I hope you don't mind that I've been puttering around in your kitchen."

"You made dinner?" she repeated, her mind still a bit slow from sex, sleep and surprise.

He grinned and nodded. "I hope it's edible."

She looked at the table again, at the flowers and candles waiting for a romantic meal for two. "I can't believe you did this."

His left eyebrow rose. "You don't like it?"

"I love it," she answered simply.

His smile returned. "Then sit down and let me serve you." He leaned over to light the tapers, then dimmed the chandelier to leave the room bathed in candlelight.

Kristin looked down at the short robe that was all she wore, aware of her bare legs and pillow-tousled hair. "Maybe I should get dressed."

"Don't go to all that trouble for my sake," he replied, holding a chair for her, his gaze lingering for a flattering length of time on her legs.

Smiling almost shyly at him, she sat down, arranging her robe around her thighs. After Perry made sure she was comfortably settled, he stepped toward the door of the kitchen. "I'll be right back."

He returned carrying the bottle of wine she'd had chilling in her refrigerator. With a flourish, he presented it to her and poured it into their glasses when she giggled and nodded approval. He then returned to the kitchen, reappearing with bowls of crisp green salads sprinkled with grated carrots and glistening with a light coating of vinegar and oil. He set her salad in front of her, then took his seat.

"This is very good," Kristin assured him after taking her first bite.

He chuckled. "Even I can't mess up a salad. At least I hope not. I haven't tasted it yet."

The salad, it turned out, was fine. Delicious, in fact. Of course, Kristin was so touched by all the trouble he'd gone to that she would have liked whatever he offered her.

He looked a bit more nervous when he brought in the main course. "I've practiced cooking a couple of times since our lesson, but I'm still pretty new at this. Don't feel you have to be polite if you don't care for it."

She smiled when she looked at the plate. "Linguini with pesto sauce? Perry, this looks wonderful."

"I brought fresh basil and pine nuts with me," he admitted. "I wasn't sure you'd have any."

She'd had both on hand, but she thought it was sweet that he'd planned ahead to do this for her. She deftly twirled a forkful of linguini and lifted it to her mouth. Perry watched anxiously as she tasted. "Well?" he asked.

"Delicious," she assured him with total honesty. "Where did you find the recipe?"

"My oldest sister gave it to me. She said it was easy enough for even a chump like me to pull off. And, by the way, she can't wait to meet you. She said any woman who could entice me into the kitchen had to be someone special."

Kristin nearly choked on the pasta she'd just swallowed. Perry had been discussing her with his family? His sister wanted to meet her?

She wasn't ready for this at all.

He seemed to read her thoughts in her expression. For a moment, his face darkened, then he deliberately lightened it with a smile. "More wine?"

She nodded, deciding not to respond to the comment about his sister.

They lingered a long time over the meal, talking quietly, laughing softly, enjoying the food and the company. Kristin still couldn't believe Perry had gone to so much trouble on her behalf. No man had ever prepared a meal for her, if she didn't count an occasional steak or burger cooked on a grill. The flowers and candles were a particularly sweet touch—a gesture that was so typical of Perry. She wondered how he had managed to get everything here without her knowledge. Had he even brought the flowers with him? If so, she was impressed that he had managed to keep everything so fresh and pretty.

During the meal, Kristin put his unsettling comment about his sister out of her mind, telling herself he'd only been making conversation. Perry was surely no more prepared for a serious, meet-the-families relationship than she was. The step they *had* taken that day was dramatic enough. Every once in a while, the intimacy they had shared simmered between them, causing them to stop speaking in midsentence, their gazes locking across the table, forks suspended in midair. And then one of them would look away, breaking the moment, and everything would be comfortable again.

When their plates were empty, Perry suggested that they move to the living room. He'd brought dessert, but they agreed to wait a little while before eating it. They carried their refilled wineglasses into the other room, where Perry again dimmed the lights and then touched a button on her CD player. Apparently, he'd preloaded it with blatantly seductive music. Kristin almost groaned when Ella Fitzgerald began to croon, "Isn't it romantic."

If Perry was trying to guarantee that she would never forget a moment of this magical evening, he was certainly succeeding. When he drew her into his arms and began to sway in time to the music, she wondered if she would forever compare every other interlude with this one.

He placed her hands on his shoulders and slid his own lingeringly down the sides of her satin robe, shaping her curves through the thin, slick fabric. She might as well have been wearing nothing at all from the way she reacted to him.

Perry rested his cheek against her hair, leading her into a slow turn. "I love dancing with you," he murmured. "You feel so good in my arms."

She smiled and stroked her hand over his broad shoulder. "I would accuse you of trying to seduce me, but you already have."

"I'm not trying to seduce you. I'm simply enjoying you."

She sighed. "You're seducing me, anyway."

He chuckled a bit gruffly. "I would have said it was the other way around."

Kristin rather liked hearing that. She pressed a bit closer to him, letting her unbound breasts brush against his chest. His eyes darkened. His voice was half an octave deeper when he spoke again. "You're a wicked woman, Kristin Cole."

"I'm not, really," she admitted. "But it feels good to be wicked every once in a while."

"Does it?"

She pressed a kiss to his throat. "Yes."

He lifted her face to look up at him. "Feel free to be as wicked with me as you like," he offered gravely.

She laughed and snapped her teeth in a mock bite. "You might be sorry you said that."

"I'm a big boy," he said, paraphrasing her earlier words. "I know what I'm doing."

Pressing closer, she felt him harden against her. "Yes," she murmured. "You certainly are a big boy."

His laugh was choked. "Definitely wicked," he muttered, sliding his hands to her hips.

Their feet were barely moving now, their bodies swaying slowly in rhythm with the sultry music. Perry lowered his head to brush his lips across her nose. "The cutest nose I've ever seen."

His compliments on her nose amused her. She might have expected him to try to woo her with flowery words about her eyes or her skin. Her lips, maybe. But her very ordinary nose?

"I like your dimples," she confessed. "I noticed them while you were on stage in New York."

"These dimples were the bane of my youth. You wouldn't believe how much teasing I endured because of them."

"Mmm." Tongue in cheek, she studied his handsome face. "I'll bet they haven't been such a handicap since you passed puberty."

The endearing slashes deepened. "There have been times when they came in handy."

"I'll just bet they have." For some reason, she found herself thinking of Jennifer, the beautiful woman she'd met at the fund-raiser ball—the one she'd sensed had been intimately involved with Perry in the past. But *how* intimately involved? And how far in the past? Two questions she didn't even want to ponder just now.

He lowered his head to kiss her again. "If my dimples were what made you bid on me during that bachelor auction, then I'll always be grateful for them."

Putting all thoughts of anyone else out of her mind, Kristin wrapped her arms around Perry's neck and pressed fully against him, removing whatever minute distance that might have remained between them. A detached part of her mind noted that a new song was playing—Linda Rondstadt's version of "What'll I Do?"

"What will I do when you're gone?" the song lyrics inquired. And that was something else Kristin didn't want to think about.

She drew back and took his hand. "I'm ready for dessert now," she said huskily.

"I brought chocolate cake."

She shook her head and allowed the sash of her robe to loosen, revealing more than a glimpse of the skin beneath. "That wasn't what I had in mind."

Before she knew quite how it happened, Kristin found herself swept off her feet, held high in Perry's arms. "Then allow me to make an alternate suggestion," he said, already moving toward the bedroom.

Laughing and clutching his shoulders, she was quite certain that whatever he suggested would be more than satisfactory.

"OPEN YOUR MOUTH."

In response to Perry's instruction, Kristin parted her lips. She closed her eyes with a moan of appreciation when he slid a piece of sinfully rich chocolate cake into her mouth. They sat cross-legged on her bed, a plate of cake between them, the only light in the room coming from the candles flickering on the twin nightstands. Kristin wore nothing but a sheet and the horseshoe bracelet. Perry had on a pair of dark blue boxer shorts—and looked spectacular in them.

Kristin had no idea what time it was. She knew only that it was sometime after midnight. She had no interest in looking at a clock. The hours that had passed since Perry arrived on her doorstep had been the most blatantly sensual interlude Kristin had ever experienced, and she wanted nothing, including time, to intrude on them.

"You have chocolate on your face," he informed her, leaning closer.

She started to reach up to wipe it away, but he caught her hand. "I'll get it," he murmured.

He touched his tongue to the corner of her mouth. And that quickly, as incredible as it was, she wanted him again.

She shook her head slowly. "Why do I feel as though you've waged a very careful campaign to get me here, like this?" Completely unable to resist him.

He chuckled, amused by her wording. "Maybe I have. I'm very good at campaigning."

"So I've heard. It seems to be a special talent of yours." And one that worried her a great deal, she could have added.

He lifted one sleek, bare shoulder, the sinuous movement only making her want him more. "I like a challenge," he murmured. "And I don't like to lose. And I'm especially tenacious when the outcome is of personal importance to me. You," he added with a smile that was so endearingly sweet her heart melted, "are important to me."

Before she could regain her voice to attempt a reply, he drew a fingertip along the line of her jaw. "Oops," he murmured, renewed arousal deepening his voice. "I'm afraid I've gotten chocolate on you again."

She arched her neck. "Then you'd better get it off."

He nibbled and licked his way from her ear to her chin, not missing a spot.

Though her hand was unsteady by the time he gravely pronounced her clean again, Kristin deliberately dipped a finger into the frosting of the slice of cake resting on the plate between them. "I do believe there's chocolate on your face, too."

"Where?" he asked with a smile of anticipation.

She traced the chocolate across his lower lip. "Here," she whispered, and then slowly kissed it away.

She decided right then that there was no taste more delicious than chocolate and Perry. If she could bottle it...she wouldn't make a dime, she decided ruefully. She could never bring herself to share that taste with anyone else.

Shifting the plate out of the way, Perry lowered her slowly back to the pillows, tugging the sheet away from her breasts in the process. "I was afraid of this," he said ruefully.

"What?"

He trailed a chocolate-covered finger around her right nipple. "I seem to have made a terrible mess with this cake."

"Then you'd better make sure you clean it up very thoroughly," she ordered him sternly.

He set the plate out of the way. "Trust me," he assured her, lowering his head. "I won't miss a crumb."

And he didn't.

KRISTIN WOKE BEFORE PERRY did the next morning. She lay for several long minutes just looking at him, amazed that such a spectacular male was sleeping in her bed. And then she slipped quietly from beneath the sheets and tiptoed into the bathroom, where she spent several moments looking in the mirror to see if the night had changed her outwardly as much as it had inwardly. She couldn't see any discernible differences. She wondered if anyone else would.

Dressed hastily in shorts and a T-shirt, her hair still damp from her shower, Kristin tiptoed through the bedroom, noting with amusement that Perry was still dead to the world. She hoped he didn't have anywhere he had to be that morning; she didn't have the heart to wake him when he was sleeping so soundly.

Carrying a cup of coffee into her office, she sat down at the computer and went through her usual morning routine of checking her e-mail. As usual, she had quite a few messages—notes from writer friends scattered around the country, a few annoying "spam" messages, a couple of writer's newsgroup digests, and a note from her agent. She read the ones that interested her, replied when necessary, stored the rest for later, then switched to her word-processing program. Maybe she'd get a little work done before Perry woke, she thought.

As was her habit, she pulled out her notebook to thoroughly outline the next chapter before she began to write it. Within minutes, she was lost in her work, her unique shorthand filling page after page of the notebook.

Something seemed to have inspired her that morning.

PERRY ENJOYED WAKING UP in Kristin's bed. The faint echo of the floral fragrance he associated with her tickled his nose even before he opened his eyes. Warm sunlight, filtered through sheer curtains on the windows, bathed his bare chest. Her sheets were soft and comfortable beneath him. The only thing missing, he decided, opening his eyes and looking at the empty pillow next to him, was Kristin.

Just as well, he thought with a rueful smile as he stretched and groaned a bit. He'd gotten a bit carried away last night. Sometimes his body had an inconvenient habit of reminding him he wasn't as young as he used to be—like now, he thought with a self-deprecating chuckle when his right knee, damaged in a high school football game, popped when he climbed out of her bed.

Pulling on his boxers to preserve her modesty— if she had any left after last night—he padded into the bathroom, which was also empty. A glance in the mirror told him a shower would be in order before he greeted her this morning. He turned on the water and stepped beneath the blessedly hot spray, thinking how nice it would be if she decided to join him.

There he went again, thinking like a horny kid. Damn, it felt good, he thought with a grin that felt goofy even to him. He was humming beneath his breath when he reached for the soap.

Leaving his hair wet, finger-combed away from his face, he donned clean slacks and shirt after the shower. He'd brought his overnight bag in from the car late last night—or early this morning, more precisely—so he'd been able to shave and brush his teeth. Now he was eager to see Kristin again— to see how she reacted to him now that they'd become lovers. She'd been so wonderfully responsive to him during the night, so open to him, he hoped she wouldn't try to keep him at a distance again today. She wouldn't have made love with him if she hadn't finally begun to trust him, at least partially—would she?

He half expected to find her in the kitchen. Or sitting out on the deck with her coffee.

He found her, instead, in her office, sitting at her desk. The notebook he'd grown to recognize and to dread was open in front of her, and she moved her pen steadily across the pages, her expression wholly absorbed in her work.

She'd never even heard him enter the room.

He cleared his throat. She didn't look up. "Kristin," he said, a bit loudly.

She didn't jump, but looked up with a slightly dazed expression, her mind obviously still focused on whatever she'd been writing in her notebook. "Yes?"

He gave her a smile. "Good morning."

"Morning. There's coffee in the kitchen. Help yourself." She glanced back down at the notebook.

This wasn't exactly the greeting he'd expected. He'd hoped for eagerness, had been prepared for a bit of shyness, but being taken completely for granted was something he hadn't counted on at all. She acted as if she hardly even realized he was there.

"Won't you join me?" he asked.

"I'll be there in a minute. I just want to finish this thought before it escapes me." Already she was writing again.

Since he seemed to have no other choice, Perry headed for the kitchen, a bit disgruntled that he was doing so alone. It seemed to him that her notes could wait at least until after breakfast. What was she writing so feverishly, anyway—her impressions of his lovemaking techniques?

He told himself to stop being paranoid. There was no reason to believe her writing had anything to do with him. He'd been told creative types tended to get lost in their own worlds at times, and he should be understanding of that if he intended to be involved with a writer—and he was most certainly involved with one particular writer.

He poured a cup of coffee and carried it out onto the deck, figuring Kristin would join him there when she was ready. Settling into one of the big spring rockers, he sipped his coffee and watched the birds and squirrels until it suddenly dawned on him exactly what he was doing. He was sulking because Kristin was ignoring him for her work. How many times, he wondered with a wince, had Jennifer complained about him doing that very same thing to her?

Elspeth's comment whispered through his mind. *If you'd paid this much attention to Jennifer, you'd be a married man now.*

He'd been behaving like a jerk, he thought regretfully. He pictured Kristin hard at work on her book—the book she'd confided to him that had been so stressful for her. She'd been surrounded by the gifts he'd given her. Her lips had still been slightly swollen from a night of his kisses. He had been a real clod to be irked that she'd spent a few minutes concentrating on her work.

By the time she joined him fifteen minutes later, he was able to greet her with a warm, easy smile. "Good morning again."

He noted that her own smile was tentative, and

that she had a tight grip on her coffee cup. "Um...I owe you an apology, I think."

He managed a look of mild surprise. "Whatever for?"

"I was rather rude to you when you greeted me earlier. I'm sorry, I should have taken more time to talk to you. I'm afraid I'd gotten distracted with an idea for my book and I—"

"Kristin." He interrupted her firmly, as if he'd hardly noticed her inattention. "I, of all people, certainly understand the responsibilities of a career. I've kept you from your work long enough as it is."

She looked a bit surprised, then pleased. "Thank you for understanding," she said. "There have been...other people who found my occasional lapses into what I call 'writer's fever' very difficult to accept."

Her former lover, perhaps? Perry mentally patted himself on the back for so neatly avoiding that unhappy comparison. He waved a hand to dismiss the subject, satisfied that she was with him now. "I thought about making breakfast for us, but since I've already cooked the only meal I've learned how to make for you..."

She laughed softly, a pleasant reward for his patience. "I'll make breakfast," she assured him. "You can help."

He sprang to his feet. "I would be delighted."

Things really were proceeding quite nicely between him and Kristin Cole, he thought a bit smugly.

10

IT WAS WELL OVER AN HOUR later by the time they had prepared and eaten breakfast and were stacking the dishes into the dishwasher. Kristin didn't remember feeling quite so relaxed in a long time. Her work had gone very well that morning and she had just breakfasted with a drop-dead gorgeous man. All in all, it was turning out to be a great day.

And then the telephone rang.

Noting that Perry was elbow-deep in dishwater, Kristin lifted the kitchen receiver. "Hello?"

"Um...Kristin?"

She didn't recognize the woman's voice. "Yes?"

"This is Elspeth Moore. I don't know if you remember me, but..."

Kristin instantly pictured the lovely woman a newsmagazine had identified as Perry's "frequent companion." "Of course I remember you. You're Perry's business associate."

She heard Perry groan.

"Yes. I'm sorry to disturb you, but I can't get an answer on his cell phone and yours was the number he gave in case we needed to reach him. Is he there?"

Kristin was aware of the irony of Perry giving

out her phone number when he rarely used it himself. But she said only, "Yes, he's here."

"Would you mind if I speak to him? I'm afraid it's rather urgent."

"Of course." She held out the phone to Perry, who was wiping his hands on a paper towel. "It's Elspeth Moore. She said it's urgent."

He nodded grimly and lifted the receiver to his ear. "It had damned well better be urgent," he growled.

Kristin turned and left the kitchen to give him his privacy. She wandered into the bedroom, where she gathered her strewn clothing from the floor and straightened the bedcovers. All evidence of their rather decadent night had been removed by the time Perry joined her. She could tell from the expression on his face that the call had not pleased him. "What's wrong?"

"Remember the reason I had to cut our bachelor auction weekend short?"

She nodded. "You said there'd been a crisis in California with one of your candidates. You said it was manufactured by his political opponents."

Perry nodded grimly. "The whole thing has cropped back up, this time with even more evidence against Leo—my candidate. It's going to get ugly. I have to be there."

"What has happened?"

Scowling, Perry explained. "It's being said that Leo has siphoned campaign money into his personal accounts. He's being accused of taking illegal contributions and of tax evasion. Elspeth said his opponent claims to have papers to back up his accusations but hasn't made them public yet."

Kristin twisted her fingers in front of her, suddenly wishing she knew a bit more about politics so she could discuss this intelligently. Instead, all she could think of to say was a lame "That sounds...bad."

Perry nodded. "It's bad."

She took a breath, phrasing her question carefully. "Is it possible your candidate really *is* guilty?"

A flicker of what might have been anger crossed Perry's face, but Kristin didn't think it was directed at her. At least, she hoped it wasn't.

"No," he said flatly. "It isn't possible. I've told you before that I choose my candidates carefully. If I thought he was capable of this, I would never have taken him as a client."

"What are you going to do?"

"The first thing I have to do is go to California and talk to Leo."

"And if you find out it's all true?"

The look he gave her made her swallow.

"It isn't," he said.

She nodded, and remembered at that moment that she really hadn't known Perry all that long. She hadn't known, for example, that he could look this hard. This angrily determined. This, she thought, was the part of him that had made him a formidable political opponent. This was the side of him she didn't know at all.

He spun on one heel, reaching for his bag, his movements jerky, forcibly controlled. "I should have been more on top of this. I thought we'd put it to rest. Damn it, I don't know where my mind's been lately..." His words trailed off, as if he'd suddenly realized exactly why he'd been distracted.

Kristin bit her lip, wondering if she was being vain to think that she had interfered with his work—and if he would unfairly blame her for doing so. Jim certainly would have, she thought, then was angry with herself for thinking of her ex-lover at a time like this. She cleared her throat and motioned toward his bag. "Have you forgotten anything? Is there anything else you need before you go?"

He surprised her by catching her arm when she would have walked out of the room. "What I need," he said, leaning closer to her, "is another forty-eight hours alone with you. Minimum." He kissed her lingeringly, then drew back with visible reluctance. "But I guess I'd better go."

She suddenly had an uncontrollable urge to grab him and refuse to let him go. But she only moistened her lips and turned to leave the room, giving him privacy to prepare for his trip.

Because she didn't know what else to do, she went to her office and turned on her computer. She wrote maybe three words while Perry was in the shower. But she couldn't concentrate on her work just then. All she could think about was how nice it had been while he'd been there. And how lonely it would seem when he left.

JUST FOR THE NOISE, Kristin turned on her office television later that afternoon, hours after Perry left. She tuned in to a cable news network. The scandal involving Perry's client was one of the lead stories. She watched the report of the background information, then narrowed her eyes when the smooth-talking anchorman mentioned Perry's name.

"Campaign manager Perry Goodman has been unavailable for comment today. Sources say he has been secluded with the senator and key campaign aides and will release a statement later. Goodman, shown here in a file video with former fiancée Jennifer Craig, flew to California this morning when news of the scandal broke. It is not known if..."

Kristin didn't hear the rest of the report. Her gaze was locked on the pictures filling her TV screen—Perry in a tuxedo, the stunningly beautiful Jennifer on his arm, an enormous diamond glinting on her left hand.

Former fiancée. Kristin had guessed that there'd been a history between Perry and Jennifer, but she hadn't realized Perry had actually asked the woman to marry him.

Reports from the stock market had appeared on the screen by the time Kristin finally roused herself enough to turn off the TV. She told herself she shouldn't be so stunned by the revelation of Perry and Jennifer's past relationship. Whatever had been between them was over—and didn't concern her, anyway.

But that was what she had believed about Jim and his ex-wife, she reminded herself dully. Even though she had no reason to believe Perry was still interested in his former lover, the memory of the pain she'd suffered when Jim betrayed her was enough to make her fear that she had made another serious mistake in falling for Perry Goodman.

The news reports from the next few days didn't reassure her. The California senator seemed to be going down in flames, and his reelection campaign seemed to be over. His former political cronies were deserting him in droves, calling for his resignation and prosecution. In politics, being even peripherally connected to a disaster of this magnitude was potentially devastating.

Perry was taking his hits, too, Kristin noted. Pundits on all the political talk shows—to which she had suddenly, uncharacteristically become addicted—were questioning his intelligence in staying with his candidate, even when there was strong evidence that the candidate was a crook. Perry continued to defend the senator, saying repeatedly that the evidence had been manufactured by political enemies—an excuse that was greeted with disbelief and outright mockery in some quarters. There were even suggestions that Perry was as crooked as his candidate, that he had covered for Leo on many occasions, that he had even accepted part of the illegally raised money as a payoff for his cooperation.

Kristin listened to all those accusations in dismay. How had this happened? Just last week, Perry had been the media's golden boy. Now, simply because of his loyalty to his friend and candidate, he seemed to have become their whipping boy.

Was Perry's loyalty displaced? The evidence against the senator looked bad. Kristin had no doubt that Perry was a very intelligent man. Could he really be so badly mistaken? Or—she winced as the thought occurred to her as she sat at her desk unable to think about anything but his professional crisis—was it possible that the pundits were right? That Perry really *was* more involved in the senator's shenanigans than he had admitted?

Though everything inside Kristin refused to accept even the possibility that Perry wasn't entirely honest and scrupulous, she couldn't help thinking of how blasé he seemed to be about money and political favors. The limos and private jet he'd provided for their charity date. The exclusive lunch on Capitol Hill. The frequent visits to her, which involved airfare and rented cars. Perry was a man at ease with spending money, who made no secret that he enjoyed the wheeling and dealing of politics, that he thrived in the spotlight.

He was risking a great deal to remain at the senator's side, if the television experts were to be believed. If Perry went down with his candidate, it could seriously affect his future desirability as a campaign strategist. After all, politicians wanted to be allied with winners, not losers. Wasn't that an indication that Perry was motivated by loyalty and friendship, and not his own best interests?

And yet—she remembered him telling her that he thrived on challenges, and that he didn't like to lose. How much was his own pride and ego tied into his candidate's fate?

How could she know whether he was also a man who could be trusted? Was he a hero for making a stand he believed in—or a scoundrel who was more obsessed by winning than being right?

The telephone on her desk rang, making her jump and rest a hand over her heart. She hadn't realized quite how far away her thoughts had taken her until she'd been startled back to the reality of her own quiet office. She picked up the receiver. "Hello?"

"Hi," his deep voice said quietly. "It's Perry."

Just hearing him made her ache.

"How are you?" she asked, concerned by how weary he sounded. "I've seen the news reports. The media has really been hounding you, haven't they?"

"Yeah. Unfortunately, it's a slow news week. No one seems to have a better story to pursue than this one."

"How can you stand it? When you left the senator's office this morning, the reporters were all over you. They shoved so many microphones in your face, and the questions they asked...I didn't know how you kept from losing your temper."

"It wasn't easy." She thought she heard anger simmering in his voice, a firmly pent-up anger that he was too consummate a politician to release in front of a hungry press.

She moistened her lips, wondering how to ask the questions that had been nagging at her since he'd left her. "Things—well, things look bad for your candidate, Perry. The press seems to have already tried him and found him guilty."

"I'm aware of that." His tone was cool, and she hoped the coolness was aimed at the media and not at her for bringing the subject up. "I hope the press will be as visible when Leo produces the evidence to clear his name."

"You've found that evidence?" Kristin asked hopefully.

"No," he said a bit too curtly. "Not yet."

"Oh." She tried to keep the doubts out of her voice, but she suspected he heard them. She tried to speak a bit more encouragingly. "I hope you find what you need soon."

You sound like a moron, Cole, she told herself with an angry, self-directed scowl.

Whatever Perry thought of her comments, he kept it masked when he said simply, "Thanks." And then he changed the subject. "How's the book coming along?"

"It's almost finished." .

"Congratulations."

"Maybe you'd better hold the congratulations until it *is* finished," she answered dryly.

"Superstitious again?" he asked, sounding as if he were trying to recapture the teasing tone he'd used with her before. "Should I send you another good-luck charm?"

"Heaven only knows where I would put another one. But thank you for the offer."

Her deliberately prim tone made him chuckle. But there was little amusement in his voice when he said, "I miss you, Kristin."

There was the briefest hesitation before she said in a rush, "I miss you, too."

And, please, Perry, don't make me regret the way I've begun to feel about you.

"I can't wait to see you again."

"When?" she asked, thinking how much easier it would be to judge his true feelings—about his candidate, and about her—if she could only talk to him face-to-face.

"I don't know. It's probably better if I don't visit you for a week or two, until some of this interest in

Leo dies down. I wouldn't want to accidentally drag you into the spotlight."

"Is that something I should worry about?" she asked, appalled by the suggestion. She knew nothing about politics, and did not want to be put in a position of having to make a comment about what was going on now.

"Not if we're careful. Once this is behind us, our relationship will only be of interest to the society columnists—not to any hard-news reporters."

"I hadn't even considered being mentioned in the society pages," she confessed. "But I guess anyone you, um, you date would be noted there. You're certainly known as a very eligible bachelor in Washington circles."

There was a sudden edge to his voice. "Don't believe everything you heard at that bachelor auction."

"So much has changed since that night," Kristin mused aloud.

"You can say *that* again."

"What will you do next—careerwise, I mean?" she asked a bit hesitantly. "Do you have other campaigns to direct?"

"I haven't finished with this one yet. Kristin, Leo did *not* accept illegal contributions, and he has not misused any campaign funds. Everything you're hearing about him is false, manufactured by a desperate and vengeful competitor. I can't prove that now—but I will. I need you to believe that."

She wanted to assure him that she believed in him implicitly. That she trusted him. But she had been hurt so badly before, and despite her anger with herself, she couldn't help but still be wary.

And everything she had seen on the news looked so incriminating toward the senator.

"You don't believe me." His voice had a flat tone to it now. If she didn't know better, she would have thought she'd hurt him with her hesitation.

"Perry, I—" She sighed. "I don't know what to believe," she admitted after a moment. "I told you I don't know anything about politics."

"This isn't about politics," he answered grimly. "This is about whether or not you've learned to trust me."

Before she could decide what to say to him, a woman's voice came clearly through an intercom, which must have been close to Perry's phone. "Mr. Goodman?"

Perry didn't bother to cover the receiver. "What is it, Anne?"

Kristin heard very clearly when the woman explained, "Jennifer Craig is on line two."

"Tell her I'll be right with her, will you?"

"Yes, sir."

"Kristin—" Perry began again.

She was the one who interrupted him this time, speaking in a rush, trying not to picture the beautiful woman she'd met at the glitzy fund-raiser—the woman who was waiting to talk to Perry. "It sounds like you're busy there. I won't keep you."

"I have a few calls to make," he admitted. "I just wanted to hear your voice."

"It was nice talking to you, too. Goodbye, Perry."

She hung up a bit too quickly, and then hid her face in her hands. She hadn't been this confused in a very long time—even when her relationship with

Jim had ended, she knew the stakes had not been this high. She had thought herself in love that time…this time she had little doubt. But had she given her love unwisely again—or had she really found a hero this time?

THIS HAD TO BE ONE of the worst weeks of his life, Perry thought glumly as he listened to the dial tone buzz in his ear. His friend was in distress, his career was in trouble, his associates had bailed out on him—all except for Elspeth and Marcus, bless their loyal, terrified hearts—and now Kristin had made it clear that after all they'd shared the past few weeks, she still hadn't learned to trust him. She still thought of him as that shallow, manipulative political player she'd described in the character sketch of Nick O'Donnell, damn it.

Well, he wasn't giving up. Not on Leo, and not on Kristin. He would defend the one and convince the other—but first he had other matters to attend to. He pressed line two on his phone. "Jennifer?"

"Hello, Perry. I hope I'm not interrupting anything."

There was a time when just the sound of her husky voice had made him want her. Now there was only one woman he wanted—a woman who wasn't sure she could trust him. "No, I just wrapped up a call. What can I do for you?"

"I wanted to let you know how sorry I am about everything that has happened with Leo. I know you were fond of him."

"I'm still fond of him, Jenn. And I still believe in him. He hasn't done anything wrong."

"Oh, Perry." She sounded thoroughly exasperated with him—something he was used to when it came to his former fiancée. "Do you always have to be so darned stubborn? You're going to ruin your career if you don't get away from this disaster now. I know you. Your career means everything to you."

"If you really knew me, you would understand that my integrity means more," he replied quietly.

She sighed. "I care very much about you, Perry. You know that. I hate to see you self-destruct this way. Everyone says Leo is going down and that you will sink with him. I had hoped I could talk some sense into you, but I should have known better. My opinion never mattered that much to you."

"You're wrong about that, too. Your opinion always mattered to me. Unfortunately, our opinions just never truly meshed. But I want you to know that I appreciate your concern."

"Would you like to get together for a drink or something, just to talk about this a little more? Maybe I can convince you how reckless you're being."

His eyebrows lifted in surprise. Suddenly Jennifer wanted to have drinks with him? She'd always resented his dedication to his career; did she think things would be different between them now that he'd encountered his biggest political challenge ever?

He declined her offer graciously. "I'm afraid I'm rather busy now. And I'll be leaving town for a while as soon as I get things settled here."

She hesitated a moment, then said, "I've heard rumors that you've been seeing the woman who 'bought' you at that charity bachelor auction."

"Those rumors are true, though I'd rather keep it out of the news for now."

"She seemed very nice," Jennifer said a bit wistfully.

"She is." Entirely too cautious when it came to him, but nice.

"I see. Well. Take care of yourself, Perry. And think about what I said, will you?"

It seemed to be the day for women to practically hang up in his ear, Perry thought as a dial tone buzzed at him from the receiver. He hung up the phone, feeling as if he'd just finally said goodbye to Jennifer and the dreams they'd once thought they'd shared.

Jennifer had once seemed to have every qualification he'd been looking for in a potential bride—brains, beauty, breeding and a deep interest in politics. But it hadn't been enough. When it came right down to it, all the things they had in common could not compensate for the things that had been missing in their relationship. Like love. Passion. Need.

Perry had always taken pride in his ability to read people, to size them up and look beyond their facades to the true characters beneath. It was that talent that had helped him align himself with an impressive string of winning, worthwhile political candidates. But with Jennifer, those instincts had failed him.

It was enough to make him start to doubt an assumption he'd had about himself for a long time. Was it possible he'd been a bit smug in his self-confidence? He glanced at the stack of articles condemning Leo and citing the so-called proof of misconduct that had been produced by the opposition. Was it conceivable that Perry had been misled again? Leo had looked him right in the eye and professed his innocence and his outrage—and Perry had believed him.

Was there any chance that he really was making a fool of himself by believing and defending Leo, stupidly destroying his own promising future in the process?

He glanced at the telephone and thought of Kristin. He'd certainly been following his instincts where she was concerned. From almost the first time he'd seen her, he had known he wanted her. By the third time he'd seen her, he'd known it was more than wanting. Sometime during the night he'd spent with her, he had decided that he would spend the rest of his life with her. And he had met her just a little more than five weeks ago.

Now he wondered if he was depending too much on those instincts that had at least once failed him. When it came right down to it, he didn't really know Kristin that well. He knew she had little interest in politics, and that she'd claimed her views were often different from his own. But just how different were they? How would he feel if it turned out she took an opposite stand on one of the issues he was truly passionate about?

He didn't know how she felt about children. He wanted kids. If men had a biological clock, his had been ticking pretty loudly lately. Marriage and family had always been in his long-range plans, which was the main reason he'd proposed to Jennifer. He'd been ready, she'd seemed suitable—it had seemed like a good idea at the time. Until she

had started pushing him to change everything that
made him who he was, making him realize what a
mistake he had made.

Perry didn't even know how Kristin felt about
him. He knew she'd started out very wary, skepti-
cal of his motives and reliability. He knew she'd
been haunted by memories of the man who'd hurt
her before, and that the experience had left her
worried about trusting unwisely again. He'd
thought he'd managed to convince her that he
wasn't like that other man. That he was a man she
could count on.

But she hadn't been able to hide the doubt in her
voice during their phone call. She wasn't convinced of the senator's innocence—was she also
questioning Perry's integrity, despite what they'd
shared?

He had thought the night they spent together
was proof that her feelings for him had changed.
That maybe she'd even fallen a little in love with
him.

But what if he was wrong?

He groaned and wearily rubbed a hand across
his face. His life hadn't been this messed up in
years. Nor his plans this uncertain. And he wasn't
quite sure what to do next. Which wasn't at all like
him.

All he knew was that he couldn't afford to lose
this time—not with Leo, and most certainly not
with Kristin.

KRISTIN FINISHED HER BOOK a week later. It was
with both satisfaction and relief that she printed
the last page. She was more than a month past

deadline, but her editor had been very understanding.

It felt good to be finished, but even better to know that the book was good. As she read through it one last time, Kristin felt a sense of satisfaction—rather surprising considering how much trouble she'd had with it. And already she was getting anxious to start her next project—an idea that had intrigued her since it had first occurred to her several weeks earlier. She tried to make it a practice to take at least a week or two off between books—time to read, shop, visit with friends, travel, generally recharge her creative batteries—but maybe this time she would just dive right in while her writing was going well.

It seemed that she had gotten past the dry spell that had affected her so painfully before, though she felt rather superstitiously as if she should knock on wood. And she had settled a few other things in her mind as she'd fleshed out her story—and her hero. She no longer doubted that the man in her book was based directly on Perry Goodman. And somehow during the process of getting to know Nick O'Donnell, she'd made up her mind once and for all about the man who had served as her model.

When her doorbell rang on Friday afternoon, she caught herself almost dashing to the door, her heart fluttering, her pulse racing like an excited schoolgirl's. Blushing at her foolishness, she made herself slow to a more dignified pace. She took a moment to compose herself at the door, running her hands through her hair, straightening the sleeveless white shirt she wore with khaki slacks, licking her lips to moisten them. Only then did she open the door, smiling—she hoped—serenely.

"Did you lose my number again?" she began, then suddenly stopped when she realized it wasn't Perry waiting outside.

"Kristin!" A blond cherub threw her arms around Kristin's waist. "Are you happy to see us?"

Automatically returning the hug, Kristin looked over the child's head to the attractive man standing behind her. Jim Hooper gave a smile that showed a lot of teeth—a smile she recognized as one meant to ingratiate. She'd seen that smile many times—back when she had been thinking about marrying this man.

11

REMEMBERING THAT KIMBERLY had asked her a question, Kristin answered mechanically. "I'm very happy to see you, Kimberly. Um—what are you doing here?"

"We came to see you. Daddy said did I want to see you and I said yes, so here we are!" Kimberly gave a big smile that revealed a couple of missing teeth.

"Aren't you going to invite us in?" Jim asked.

As if she could refuse, with his nine-year-old daughter gazing adoringly up at her—as Jim very well knew. "Of course. Come in."

Kimberly skipped past her. Jim followed more slowly. He paused beside her. "It's good to see you, Krissie. You look very nice."

He leaned over to kiss her. She neatly avoided that with a quick sidestep, turning to his daughter, instead. "Goodness, you've grown so much since I saw you last. And I think you're even more beautiful than you were before."

Kimberly nodded happily and patted her curly blond hair. "I got a haircut."

"It's lovely. Would you like a snack? I have milk and oatmeal cookies in the kitchen."

Rubbing her tummy, the child nodded enthusiastically. "I'm *starving*."

Kristin held out her hand. "We can't have that."

Kimberly took Kristin's hand and skipped along beside her to the kitchen, chattering the entire way. Jim followed.

Kristin settled the little girl at the table with cookies and milk, then turned on the small TV she kept on the kitchen counter, tuning into a cartoon channel. "Would you mind if your daddy and I talk in the living room for a few minutes, moppet?"

"Okay. I like this cartoon." Kimberly filled her mouth with cookie and stared contentedly at the flickering screen.

Kristin turned to Jim, her smile forced, her tone unnaturally sweet. "Shall we?" she asked, motioning toward the other room.

She saw him swallow before he nodded and turned toward the door.

She wasn't smiling when she turned to him in the living room. "What are you doing here, Jim?"

"It really *is* good to see you, Kristin. I've missed you."

Again, she deftly avoided an attempted kiss. "You haven't answered my question. Why are you here?"

"I wanted to see you."

She lifted an eyebrow. "And you didn't bring your wife?"

He winced. "Now, Krissie…"

"Don't call me that."

"You used to like it." His wounded look might have been endearing to her at one time—now it only annoyed her.

"I never liked it," she corrected him with some

satisfaction. "I merely tolerated it while we were seeing each other. Now I don't have to."

"You're still angry. I understand that."

His solemn, sympathetic tone only irked her more. "I'm not angry. I just don't know why you're here. And why *no one* calls before popping in anymore."

"All right, Krissie—er, Kristin, I'll level with you. My wife is on a business trip to Chicago. I'm here because you've been on my mind lately and I wanted to see you."

"And you brought Kimberly because you knew I wouldn't close the door in your face if she was with you."

"I brought Kimberly because I know what good friends the two of you were when we were together. I thought you might want to see her."

She felt her lip curl. She'd lost a great deal of respect for Jim when he'd lied to her and dumped her so unceremoniously, but she'd thought he was above using his daughter as a bribe. "As much as I enjoy seeing Kimberly, I really don't think it's a good idea for you to come here when your wife is out of town. I don't think she would like it."

Jim cleared his throat. "Well, the thing is…Linda and I have separated again, Kristin. Our reunion didn't work out at all. I was clinging to something that should have ended long ago, and I've only just begun to understand that."

She crossed her arms in front of her, hoping this wasn't leading where she knew it was leading. "I'm sorry to hear that."

"You aren't going to make this easy for me, are you."

"Jim…"

He held up both hands, palms outward. "Let me finish, honey. I know I hurt you very badly last year. That I was unforgivably cruel to you. But I hope you can forgive me. I hope we can start over."

She shook her head. "I'm afraid that's not possible."

"Don't say that, darling." He reached for her hands, taking them before she could pull away and holding them tightly. "What we had together was so good. You were crazy about Kimberly…and, I believed, about me. We were a great pair, until I ruined everything. But, don't you see? I know how wrong I was now. I'll never make that mistake again. I know it's you I want, not Linda."

"No, Jim. It isn't going to happen. You see…"

"You're a very special woman, Kristin. You're so gracious and peaceful and loving. So sweet. Linda's not happy unless her life is in turmoil. She's temperamental and tempestuous and totally unpredictable. I don't want to live that way anymore. Maybe I'm just getting too old for it. What I want is the gentle, quiet relationship you and I had."

He made her sound like a favorite pair of old slippers, Kristin thought in mounting outrage. It was without doubt the least-flattering speech any man had ever made to her, though he would probably be utterly bewildered if she let him know just how insulting she had found his words. "I think you'd better leave, Jim."

"You're still angry. I hurt you so terribly. It's going to take time for me to make it up to you, isn't it?" He nodded sagely. "Well, I deserve that. You want a courtship, you'll get one. Why don't we start with dinner tonight at that Italian restaurant you like so much? Vincenzo's, wasn't it?"

"Vincenzo's went out of business months ago—not long after you and I did," she answered bluntly. "I don't want a courtship from you, Jim. All I want is for you to—"

"I've finished my cookies," a cheery little voice announced from the doorway. "Can we walk down to the lake now, Kristin?"

Kristin bit her lip. It would be easy enough for her to throw Jim out, but obviously she couldn't do it in front of his child. "Um—"

"Sure, Kimmie," Jim said jovially, practically daring Kristin to dispute him. "Let's all walk down to the lake—just the way we used to."

Nodding happily, Kimberly slipped her hand into Kristin's. "Will we see any deer? And do you still have squirrels? Can I throw rocks in the water and look for minnows?"

Because there was absolutely nothing else she could do—for now—Kristin allowed herself to be led outside. But she gave Jim a look over his daughter's head that let him know she wasn't at all happy with him. He met her gaze with a look of such patently false innocence that she was tempted to push him into the lake when they got there. That would show him that she could be as temperamental and unpredictable as the next woman.

And then Kimberly started to sing, and Kristin knew she would do no such thing. Not in front of the child, at least.

PERRY DROVE DOWN Kristin's street with a great sense of relief that he'd made it here without attracting any undue attention. A great deal had happened since the last time he had talked to her, and now he had a few days free—and he wanted to spend them with Kristin.

He saw the blue minivan parked in her driveway and wondered who was visiting her. Maybe he should come back later, when she was alone. But, no. He was too impatient to see her. He wouldn't mind meeting some of her friends.

He rang the doorbell, but there was no answer. Frowning, he looked at Kristin's car and at the minivan, wondering where she could be.

Maybe this time he should have called first.

On an impulse, he tried the doorknob. The door wasn't locked. Poking his head inside, he saw that the living room was empty. "Kristin? Hello?" he called out loudly.

The house was silent.

He debated only a moment before entering the house, calling out her name again. He checked her office and her bedroom. Both were empty. "Kristin, it's Perry. Are you here?"

No response. Why would she have left home without locking her door? She wouldn't, of course. He looked toward the kitchen, suddenly realizing where she might be.

He noticed a plate of cookie crumbs and a partial glass of milk on the kitchen table as he passed through. Either Kristin had been indulging her inner child, or her visitor had brought a kid.

He opened the door that led out onto the deck. "Kristin?"

The spring rockers were unoccupied. But he

heard the high-pitched voice of a child coming from the direction of the lake. The voice seemed to be getting closer. Smiling, Perry leaned against the railing to wait for them, anticipating the moment when he would see Kristin again.

But when he did catch sight of her, his smile froze, then faded away.

An energetic little girl was walking at Kristin's side, her right hand held snugly in Kristin's. The child's left hand was gripped by a man who was smiling sappily at Kristin over the little girl's head.

Perry recognized them immediately as Kristin's ex-boyfriend and his daughter—the ones from the amusement park photos. The jerk who had dumped Kristin and gone back to his wife. The bastard who had hurt her so badly that Perry still hadn't been able to gain her trust.

Perry shoved his hands in his pockets to keep himself from following up on an impulse to smash the guy's grinning face in.

He had already realized how hard he had fallen for Kristin Cole. But only now did he understand that he was willing to do whatever it took to win her, even fight for her, if necessary.

No campaign had ever been more crucial to him than the one he now waged to win Kristin's heart.

Kristin looked up from the little girl and glanced toward the house. Her gaze met Perry's—and held. Her eyes widened.

He nodded coolly, knowing his determination must be written on his face.

The little girl spotted Perry only a moment later. "There's someone on your deck, Kristin," she said clearly.

Perry had the satisfaction of seeing the other man's smile vanish. "Who is that, Kristin? Has he been in your house?"

"That," Kristin said, "is my—um—my friend, Perry Goodman."

"Your friend, Kristin?" Perry stepped to the top of the steps and held his hand out to her. "Much more than that, I would say."

She hesitated before she responded. It couldn't have been more than a moment, but it felt like a very long time in which Perry's entire future seemed to hang in the balance. And then, with a spark of what might have been recklessness in her eyes, she reached for his hand. "You're right, of course. I own you. I paid ten thousand dollars for you."

He laughed in delight and relief, and drew her to his side, wrapping an arm around her shoulders. "True. And it was a one-time-only bargain sale. No refunds. No returns."

"What on earth are you talking about?" the other man asked crossly.

"Is this your boyfriend, Kristin?" the little girl asked at the same time.

"Yes," Perry answered, ignoring the man and smiling at the child. "I'm her boyfriend. And who are you?"

"I'm her friend. My name's Kimberly Hooper. This is my daddy, Jim Hooper. He's Kristin's friend, too."

Perry nodded briefly to the other man. Neither extended a hand. "It's nice to meet you both."

"You didn't tell us you had a new boyfriend,

Kristin," Kimberly commented, not seeming particularly perturbed by the oversight.

Her father didn't take the news nearly as well. "No, Kristin, you certainly didn't."

"You haven't given me a chance." Kristin smiled up at Perry. "They surprised me with a visit, and we haven't had a chance to sit down and talk yet."

"Oh? Well, maybe we can all do so now. I always enjoy meeting your friends. Would you like me to make a pot of coffee while you take them into the living room? I know where everything is, of course."

"Thanks, but that won't be necessary." Jim Hooper looked at his watch. "Kimberly and I have to be going."

"What a shame." Perry was sure the smile he gave Hooper conveyed the opposite message.

Hooper spoke pointedly to Kristin, deliberately ignoring Perry. "I still want to talk to you, Kristin. When will you be free to get together?"

"I'm afraid we're going to be very busy for some time," Kristin answered firmly, her tone as cool and detached as if she were speaking to a persistent salesperson. "Aren't we, Perry?"

He gave her a warm, intimate smile. "Yes, we have many plans."

Jim apparently knew when to concede defeat. "We'll be going now. Tell Kristin goodbye, Kimberly."

Perry watched as Kristin bade a tender farewell to little Kimberly.

"Can we come see you again, Kristin?" the child asked hopefully.

"You will always be welcome here, sweetheart,"

Kristin replied, but the hint of sadness Perry heard in her voice let him know she didn't expect to see the child again.

"Goodbye, Kristin," Jim said stiffly. "I hope you'll be happy."

"I'll make sure of that," Perry said, and for a moment he allowed the masculine possessiveness he'd been battling to show in his expression.

The other man nodded in resignation. "Come on, Kimberly. Let's go."

The child took her father's hand and waved over her shoulder. "Bye, Kristin. Bye, Mr.—er, Kristin's boyfriend."

Perry chuckled. She really was a cute kid. No wonder Kristin was so fond of her.

After he heard the minivan drive away, he turned to look at Kristin. He caught her wiping a single tear from her cheek, and he frowned. "Are you sad about Kimberly—or her father?" he demanded with uncharacteristic tactlessness.

Kristin squared her chin. "Kimberly, definitely. Seeing her again reminded me of how much I've missed her."

"And what did seeing *him* again remind you of?"

She lifted an eyebrow in response to his jealous tone, but she answered succinctly, "It reminded me of how glad I am that he went back to his ex-wife."

Perry smiled naturally again for the first time since he had seen her walking up the path with Jim and Kimberly Hooper. He was filled once again with hope—and with determination. "That's what I was hoping you would say."

He tightened his arm to pull her closer.

Kristin pulled away before he could follow through on his intention to kiss her.

"I am *not* boring!" she said, glaring fiercely at him.

"I never said you were boring. In fact…"

"I know how to have fun. I can be spontaneous."

"Okay…" he said carefully, wondering where this was leading.

"Just because I work hard at my career and don't run off to Australia on a moment's notice with handsome pilots and don't enjoy living in constant turmoil and chaos, people think I'm dull and un-adventurous. Is that what you see in me, Perry? Is your life in Washington so stressful and hectic that you come here to rest in my boring, peaceful presence?"

Her challenging tirade fascinated him. The spark of defiance in her eyes aroused him. "Where do you stand on your book?" he asked abruptly.

Still seething about whatever had set her off in the first place, she answered distractedly. "It's finished. All I have to do is proofread the printout."

He was delighted to hear that. "Then go pack a bag. I've got a couple of calls to make."

That got her attention. "Pack? What am I packing for?"

He grinned at her. "You are about to be spontaneous and adventurous. Pack casually and comfortably—and don't forget your bikini."

"I don't own a bikini," she answered repressively.

"Improvise," he suggested.

"But...what about your job? What about the crisis in California?"

"All taken care of. I'll tell you all about it later." After he found out for himself just how far her trust in him extended, he silently vowed.

"But I can't just leave. I have so many things to do. So much to—"

He lifted his eyebrows and interrupted her. "We could always stay here and watch TV or something, if you'd rather. That sounds like a quiet, peaceful weekend."

Her chin firmed and lifted. "I'll go pack."

He nodded in satisfaction. "You've got half an hour."

Big words, he told himself ruefully. He only hoped he could pull enough strings to follow through.

"I CAN'T BELIEVE I'M IN Hawaii."

Perry laughed. "That has to be the tenth time you've said that."

"I can't help it." Wrapped in bathrobes, they sat on a shaded lanai with a breeze from the ocean tousling their hair—the ocean that was only a stone's throw from where they sat. "Yesterday I was at home in North Carolina and today I woke up in Maui. This is so unlike me. The trip wasn't on my calendar. I didn't make any lists. I didn't tell anyone where I was going. It was a totally spontaneous action."

"And how does it feel?" Perry asked, watching her indulgently.

"Wonderful," she answered simply.

He smiled. "I'm glad to hear that," he said, his

body still heavy and sated from making love to her all night. "It feels damned good to me, too."

She tossed her head, letting the breeze catch her hair. "This condo is fabulous. The view is breathtaking. I can't believe you were able to make the arrangements on such short notice."

"I have a few friends in high places."

She eyed him speculatively. "They must be very good friends."

"Let's just say I called in some big favors." And now he owed a few, as well, but he would worry about that later.

"I've never been to Maui before."

"Yes, you mentioned that."

A becoming blush stained her cheeks. "I must sound very unsophisticated. You would think I'd never left the Carolina hills, the way I've been carrying on. I really have traveled a bit, but never quite like this. I've always had to have a reason to go somewhere—a conference or book tour or research trip or at least a vacation that had been planned and scheduled down to the last minute. Taking off on impulse this way—well, that's always been more my mother's style."

"And you never thought you could be like your impulsive, happy-go-lucky mother." It was a shot in the dark, but it must have hit home, he thought when Kristin's eyes widened, and she nodded.

"Mother always said I was just like my dad. He was an engineer—very methodical and practical. Mother's opposite, really, but they adored each other. She loosened him up and he took care of her."

"A responsibility you took over when he died?"

"No, not exactly," she answered, her gaze focused on the vividly blue horizon. "I always took care of myself."

She looked at him then, her eyes big and serious-looking. "I love my mother very much, Perry. I don't want you to get the idea that she wasn't a wonderful mother to me. She was always just a little…different."

"From what I've seen of her, Sophie's a jewel," he assured her. "Though I'm sure there were times you felt a bit eclipsed by her, I'm sure overall you felt very fortunate to have her for your mother."

"Exactly," she said, nodding her head and looking pleased that he understood.

"And you're not entirely unlike her," he added. "I've noticed many qualities you've inherited from your mother."

He noted an almost hopeful spark of interest in her eyes. "You have?"

"Of course. The creativity that shows in your writing. The courage it took for you to send your work out and risk rejection and criticism. The spirit of fun that made you bid on me at the bachelor auction. And you *are* here with me now."

She smiled. "Yes. I am."

Satisfied that he'd made his point, he motioned toward the beach. "Want to go for a swim?"

"Maybe in a little while. Right now I'd like to just sit back and absorb the beauty."

He stood. "Then I'll bring out some juice and fresh fruit. The kitchen is stocked with pineapple, papaya and mango."

"Sounds wonderful. Need any help?"

"No. You 'absorb the beauty.' I don't need a cooking lesson to slice fruit."

She didn't argue with him. She was already watching the ocean again, looking so relaxed and contented that he was doubly glad he'd had this brainstorm.

He was gone less than twenty minutes. But when he returned, Kristin had already located her ubiquitous notebook and was busily scribbling in it. Perry almost groaned in dismay. They were sitting here in paradise and all she wanted to do was search for words to describe it?

"Um...Kristin? Here's your fruit."

"Thank you," she said without looking up from the notebook. "I'll have some in a minute. I just want to finish this thought...."

She was gone, he thought in resignation. Completely zoned out. He could strip naked and dance the hula in front of her and her only reaction would be to write even faster as she made notes about his bizarre behavior. She was in "writer mode"—and he was learning to live with it. He just wished they could have talked a little longer before she'd drifted into her creative trance.

He still didn't know whether she trusted him enough to let herself love him.

Since he seemed to have some free time on his hands, he headed for the bedroom, thinking he'd make some phone calls and make sure all was still proceeding smoothly in California. But something had happened to him lately. He had discovered that he wasn't interested in working all the time— an admission that would probably leave some of his acquaintances reeling in shock. His priorities seemed to have changed. His career was still important to him—but other things were becoming more important, he thought as he glanced in the direction of the lanai.

A stack of neatly printed pages on the writing desk in one corner of the airy room caught his eye. Kristin had brought along the manuscript she had just finished writing; he assumed she'd thought there might be time to proofread it during their trip. It was long past time he familiarized himself with her writing, he thought, taking a seat at the desk and pulling the pages in front of him. Maybe he would learn something about Kristin in the process.

12

KRISTIN SET HER NOTEBOOK aside and stretched, feeling her muscles protest with the movement, which meant, she thought ruefully, she'd been sitting in one position too long. She did that sometimes when she got carried away with an idea. Something in the Hawaiian air must have started her creative juices flowing. Something...

She suddenly gasped and sat straight up in her chair. Hawaii. She was still sitting on the lanai, and the scenery was as beautiful and romantic as ever. But the man who had brought her to this gorgeous, exotic place was nowhere to be seen. She had drifted into her fantasies and totally ignored him.

She would be lucky if he hadn't boarded a plane back to the mainland and left her sitting there alone with her notebook and a view she'd been too distracted to appreciate for the past...two hours, she thought with a wince, glancing at her watch. Which only went to prove that she was nothing at all like her fun-loving, impetuous mother. Sophie wouldn't have spent two hours of an impulsive tropical vacation with a handsome man writing in a notebook about an imaginary hero—even if the imaginary hero she'd come up with for her next book also shared a suspicious number of characteristics with the real-life man in question.

She stood, mentally practicing her apology, and went into the condo to find Perry. Jim, she thought with a wince, would have been waiting for her in cold silence, hurt and disappointed that she'd ignored him so rudely. She knew that from painful experience. She braced herself for a similar reaction from Perry.

She found him in the bedroom. The double doors on either side of the airy room were open, letting a brisk, deliciously scented breeze flow through. Wearing nothing but a pair of khaki shorts, Perry lay on his stomach on the bed, propped on his elbows, her manuscript pages scattered in front of him. *Her* manuscript, she realized with a kick of nerves. She twisted her fingers in front of her. "Perry?"

He didn't seem to hear her at first, so she said his name again, a bit more loudly.

Looking up, he focused on her, then set the page in his hand aside. His movements deliberate, he swung his legs over the side of the bed and stood.

Feeling awkward and uncertain of his mood, she tightened the sash on her robe as he moved toward her. "I'm afraid I got carried away with my notes and let the time slip away from me. I'm sorry I…"

Before she could finish the sentence, his mouth was on hers. The rest of the apology was lost in a kiss that nearly short-circuited every synapse in her brain.

By the time Perry finally drew back for air, Kristin was clinging to him helplessly, her knees almost too weak to support her. "What…?"

"I love your book."

"Oh. Well, I'm…"

He kissed her again. "It was wonderful," he murmured against her lips. "Very illuminating."

She could think of absolutely nothing to say. What had he found in those pages to make him react so dramatically? She wondered nervously just what he had found so illuminating.

He was grinning like a fool—which she found as endearing as it was baffling. "I'm about ten pages from finishing it. I still don't know who the blackmailer is. Why don't you put me out of my misery and tell me?"

At the moment, she was finding it hard to remember anything about the book. "I—"

He frowned and shook a finger at her, still oddly buoyant. "Come on, don't be stubborn. Tell me who the bad guy is."

It seemed easier to play along with him than to try to figure out what he was thinking at the moment. She managed a smile. "You'll just have to read it for yourself."

He nuzzled her temple, smiling against her skin. "C'mon, Kristin. Tell me who it is. You don't want me to waste any more time reading when you and I could be…"

"Wasting time?" Though her pulse was rocketing like crazy, she lifted an eyebrow in a coolly insulted manner. "Excuse me, did you just say reading my book is wasting time?"

"Definitely not," he assured her. "It's just that the story is so extremely fascinating I simply can't wait any longer to find out how it ends. So I was hoping you would take pity on me and…"

"Forget it."

His expression turned sly, a look of challenge in

his beautiful eyes. "I have ways of making you talk," he murmured, pulling her closer.

Though she would bet he felt her heart rate speed up beneath his fingertips, she managed to keep her chin high, her voice steady and amused. "Do what you will to me. You'll never make me talk."

"Oh, I wouldn't bet on that." His hand slipped lower, slowly parting the fabric of her robe. She shivered when the breeze brushed over her skin, though it wasn't at all cold.

Loosened, the robe slipped from her shoulders. She moved to stop it, but Perry's hands were in the way. The robe slid down her arms, the sash falling away. She wore nothing beneath it but a pink silk teddy.

"Tell me who the bad guy is," Perry murmured, his hands already sliding from her waist upward.

"No." Her voice wasn't quite as firm this time.

He cupped her breasts in his hands, lifting them so that they almost spilled out of the lacy top of her teddy. Lowering his head, he nuzzled between them, his breath warm on her flesh. "Tell me."

She caught her breath. "No."

His tongue slipped beneath the lace barely covering her right breast to flick the distended nipple beneath. His left hand moved downward, over her stomach to the sensitive area beneath. The thin fabric dampened beneath his ministrations. Kristin clutched at his bare shoulders as her knees weakened.

"Are you going to tell me now?" he demanded, lowering her to the bed.

She had forgotten the question. "Tell you what?"

He loomed above her, his weight on one knee, his arms propped on either side of her head. "Tell me you want me," he murmured against her mouth.

"I want you," she repeated readily.

"That you're very glad you met me."

"I am very glad I met you," she whispered as his mouth trailed down her throat.

His voice was a low rumble in his chest, vibrating against her breast. "That's all I wanted to know. For now."

She couldn't help laughing huskily. "I thought you wanted to ask about my book."

The manuscript slid from the bed to cascade chaotically on the carpet. Kristin didn't care—the pages were numbered, and she could always print out another copy. At the moment, she had something much more important on her mind.

"I'll find out the ending for myself," Perry vowed. "Later."

"*Much* later," she agreed, pulling him down to her.

THE NEXT THREE DAYS were without doubt the most exhilarating interlude of Kristin's life, filled with new experiences—and copious notes for future books. She hiked through a rainforest, snorkeled through schools of beautiful, colorful fish, went sailing and parasailing, tasted exotic foods at a moonlight luau, donned a grass skirt and attempted a hula, and rode horseback on a beach.

And she fell even more deeply in love with Perry Goodman than she had been before.

She couldn't have created a more perfect companion if she'd pulled one directly from her most intimate fantasies. He was considerate, courteous, charming. Incredibly patient with her occasional attacks of nerves. And the most stimulating, satisfying lover she could ever have imagined. There was no holding back with him, no maintaining a safe distance. Perry threw himself wholeheartedly into everything they did during those days. *Everything*.

"I've never felt so daring and adventurous," she admitted to Perry as they walked hand-in-hand at midnight on the beach outside their condo. "These have been the most exciting few days of my life. I hate for them to end."

"Then don't let them end," he answered promptly, his hand tightening on hers. "Make them last a lifetime. Marry me."

She promptly stumbled on the sand, nearly falling flat on her face. Perry reached out to steady her, but she regained her footing as she turned to stare at him. Surely he was joking, she thought dazedly. But he wasn't smiling, and the familiar spark of mischievous humor was missing from his eyes.

She tried to remember how many glasses of wine he'd had for dinner. But he was walking steadily, and he didn't seem inebriated. So it couldn't be that.

She had to have misunderstood what he said. "Did you say…?"

"I asked you to marry me," he clarified evenly.

"If you want to be really adventurous, we'll leave Hawaii as husband and wife."

Maybe *she* was the one who'd had too much to drink. Two glasses of wine with dinner, and a glass of champagne in the dance lounge afterward. She didn't usually drink that much. "Surely you aren't serious."

"Why not?"

"It's too soon to even think about taking a step like that. We've known each other barely two months."

"How many months does it take to fall in love?" he asked logically.

"L-love?"

"Love," he repeated, his voice firm. "You should be familiar with the word, since your work makes you sort of an expert on the subject."

She shook her head. "Those are books. Fiction. Fantasy. You're talking about real life—and I'm far from an expert in that."

He caught her hands and squeezed them reassuringly. "Then we'll learn together. Think what a grand adventure that will be."

"Marriage isn't a sport, Perry," she retorted curtly. "It isn't a game. It's serious. Permanent." *Terrifying.*

"It's all of those things. Of course, it should be fun, as well. And fulfilling. And challenging. And stimulating. You and I can make it everything we want it to be."

She lifted both hands to her head, pressing against her temples, trying to decide whether what she was feeling was dismay...or temptation. "There's really no reason to continue this discussion tonight," she said, deciding not to take any chances. "It's much too soon to start talking about marriage."

"Okay, fine," he said equably. "If you're more comfortable taking a safe, cautious path, we'll handle it that way. You set the schedule, make a list or an agenda, or whatever you like, and let me know the details. Choose a date for me to tell you that I love you, another date for us to discuss a possible engagement—or going steady, if you'd like to take it even more slowly. And then—"

She pulled her hands out of his. "You're making fun of me."

"Not making fun. Teasing a little, perhaps. You've suddenly become so organized and conservative again."

"That's because you've started to discuss something very important to me," she replied. "I can't joke about marriage. I can't take marriage as lightly as an impulsive vacation."

His smile vanished. "And neither do I," he assured her. "I didn't propose to you on impulse, Kristin. This is something I've considered very carefully."

"When?" she demanded bluntly.

"Since the night I met you," he answered simply. "Since the first time you smiled at me and wrinkled your nose at me. Since the first time I kissed you. It's something I've thought about for all the weeks we've known each other."

She was stunned. "I didn't know—"

"You thought I made a habit of constantly rearranging my schedules so I could show up on women's doorsteps? That I've been hopping planes and renting cars and delegating responsibilities because I was hoping for more cooking lessons?"

"I had no idea you were thinking about marriage."

"Of course I was. I'm thirty-six years old, Kristin. I'm too old for casual affairs. I'm ready to move on. I was briefly engaged a year ago, but it fell apart because we weren't right for each other. I know now what I want. I want you."

She frowned. Was that it? Was Perry simply ready to get married and had pragmatically decided she was a suitable match? She wasn't sure she liked that possibility any more than her previous suspicion that he had proposed on a romantic impulse.

He took her hands again. "Kristin, don't try to tell me you don't love me. I know you do. I read it in your book."

She gaped at him. "You did *what?*"

She was absolutely certain that nowhere in the pages Perry had read had it said, "Kristin Cole is in love with Perry Goodman." At least, she hoped it didn't say that. The way her mind had been wandering lately, it was entirely possible that her fingers *had* hit those keys.

"Don't tell me that Nick O'Donnell isn't based on me," he warned her. "I know he is."

"Well, he…"

He nodded in satisfaction, as if she'd confirmed his accusation. "At the beginning of the story, your heroine, Amy, thinks Nick is shallow and vain and spoiled. Which is exactly what you thought of me when you first met me…don't deny it."

"I didn't intend to," she answered dryly, her heart beating so hard in her chest she wondered if he could hear it. She struggled for a nonchalant tone. "But I still don't see what makes you think I—"

"By the end of the book, Amy looks beyond the surface. She realizes that he can be trusted. That he understands the concepts of loyalty and commitment, that his word is his bond. That he is willing to make sacrifices for what he truly believes in, even if he is the only one who believes."

Kristin was both flattered that he'd read her work so closely and anxious about him finding himself there. He'd concluded from her writing that she had fallen in love with him—and he was right. But she still didn't know how he felt about her.

"I…um…" She flexed her fingers in his, trying to think of what to say.

"You haven't asked about Leo. Not once, did you know that?"

She blinked, her mind spinning. What did the senator have to do with this? "I…um…"

"He's been cleared of all charges. Entirely. Did you know?"

She gasped. "No. I hadn't heard."

He nodded as if in satisfaction. "I didn't think you had. It wouldn't have hit the airwaves until today—and I know you haven't seen any news today."

"But—how?"

"He was being set up. We hired a private investigator who proved it. Already his political cronies are rallying around him again, telling him they knew all along that he was innocent." His mouth twisted in irony as he finished.

Kristin tightened her hands around his, a lump forming in her throat. Perry's faith in his friend hadn't been misplaced. He wouldn't suffer for his loyalty. "Perry, I'm so pleased for you. I know how much this means to you."

He lifted her hands to his mouth and pressed a quick kiss against her knuckles. "You believed in me, didn't you? You had your doubts about Leo—and that's understandable, since you've never even met him—but you believed in me."

"I knew you really believed in his innocence, if that's what you're asking," she whispered. "When I heard other people hinting that you have no real principles, that you'll say or do anything to win a campaign—well, I knew they were wrong. They didn't know you at all."

"That's what I realized when I read your book. You weren't sure about my candidate—but you know me. And you love me."

There seemed to be no reason to deny it now. Perry had figured it all out too well. "Yes," she said simply.

"And I love you, too. I have from the beginning, I think."

Her eyes instantly filled with tears. "Perry…"

"I love you, Kristin." He kissed her lingeringly. "Say you'll marry me."

Fear clutched her chest, squeezing her heart. "I—I love you, too, Perry. But…I need a little more time, okay?"

She could tell he wanted to argue. "Why?"

"I'm really not the spontaneous type," she admitted ruefully. "I need time to think about this. To digest the things we've said." She needed time to decide if a marriage could possibly survive between a very public, very polished, very perfect politician and a somewhat reclusive writer who had no interest in politics and a tendency to drift into creative trances.

Though it was obvious he didn't want to concede, Perry nodded gravely. "You have all the time you need," he assured her. "I'm not going anywhere. But, Kristin?"

"Yes?"

He brushed his lips against hers. "Don't make me wait too long."

PERRY'S PROPOSAL EFFECTIVELY put an end to the vacation. He and Kristin both had to return to their responsibilities at their respective homes, and they couldn't put it off any longer. Without another word about marriage—but after one last night of especially spectacular lovemaking—they left the island, keeping their regrets about doing so to themselves.

Kristin managed not to shed a tear as the plane left the runway.

A stack of mail and a dozen telephone messages were waiting for her when she returned home, exhausted from the long flights. She checked through them while Perry made a few calls of his own. When he finished, they looked at each other somberly.

"I have to get back to Washington," he said.

"I have to get back to work," she agreed.

They both sighed.

They had coffee and sandwiches before he left, but both were aware of passing time. Afterward, Kristin walked Perry to the door.

He studied her face for a long moment. And then he reached out to touch her cheek. "You look so serious," he said with a faint smile. "You have ever since our talk on the beach."

She swallowed and nodded. "It was a, um, very serious talk."

"Yes." His thumb traced her lower lip. "I don't suppose you've come up with any answers."

"No. I just need a little more time," she repeated lamely.

"All the time you need," he assured her. And then grinned. "But hurry."

She smiled a little in response to his quip, not taking her eyes off his face. He was such a beautiful man. Perfectly groomed, as usual. He still looked to her as if he could have stepped off the cover of one of her books. Though she had never considered herself so shallow as to be overly influenced by outward appearance, she couldn't help remembering the way she'd reacted the first time she'd seen Perry. She had definitely been struck by his looks—as had nearly every other woman in the crowded hotel ballroom. But she'd found since then that there was so much more to him than his handsome face.

And he wanted to marry her.

His thumb moved across her lower lip again. "I love you, Kristin. But I have to go."

Her eyes burning, she nodded. "I know," she whispered.

"You'll think about my proposal?"

"I can't imagine I'll be thinking about much else," she confessed ruefully.

He smiled. "Good."

And then he kissed her until she could hardly think at all.

PERRY WAS HAVING ONE HELL of a day. It was a suffocatingly hot afternoon in Washington, and the office air conditioner had died unexpectedly that morning. Frantic calls to repair contractors had elicited only promises that someone would be there "soon"—which could mean anything from two hours to two weeks. Reporters had been calling all day, still wanting quotes from him about how deeply he had believed in Leo all along, and how disgusted he was with the opponent's unconscionable efforts to destroy Leo's political future.

He hadn't talked to Kristin in days. Every time he'd called her, he'd gotten her answering machine. She hadn't returned his messages. The few calls they'd had before she'd dropped out of sight had been vague and unsatisfying, leaving him no closer to knowing what her answer would be than he had been the night he proposed to her. If he hadn't been so inundated with responsibilities that affected too many people other than himself, he would have dropped everything and gone after her.

He missed her, he thought glumly, pushing his shirtsleeves up his arms in a vain attempt to cool off. It had been almost two weeks since their vacation in Hawaii, and he missed her so badly there was a constant ache inside him.

If there had been any doubt in his mind before

that he loved her—which there hadn't—it would have vanished during these past few days.

Elspeth walked into the room with a stack of message slips. Though she was as poised and well-groomed as ever, there was a sheen of moisture on her fair skin, and a deep flush on her cheeks. She'd shed the jacket that matched her sleeveless sheath, but that was her only concession to the stifling heat in the offices, unlike Perry, who'd ditched his jacket and tie and opened the top two buttons of his shirt.

"These have to be returned immediately," she said, setting two messages apart from the others. "The rest can be at your convenience."

He nodded and ran a hand through his hair. He felt the damp strands stick to his fingers.

Elspeth winced. "Perry—check your hand."

He looked down automatically, and groaned at what he saw. For some strange reason, his pen had started to leak. Black ink was all over his hand, his shirt...and now, presumably, his forehead. "Tell me it's not all over my face."

Elspeth smiled sympathetically. "You'd better go wash up before making your calls."

"Damn it, what else can go wrong today?" he demanded, shoving impatiently away from his desk.

"Please don't ask that," Elspeth begged with exaggerated nervousness. "I'm afraid to think what could happen."

"It couldn't possibly get any worse than this," he said, trying to respond with his usual humor. As he spoke, he swung a hand in emphasis—and promptly knocked over a tall stack of files that had been sitting on his desk. Papers flew everywhere.

Elspeth started to laugh. "Honestly, Perry, what is with you today? I've never seen you like this. You're a mess...in more ways than one."

"Tell me about it. All I need now is a herd of reporters at the door with cameras to show my humiliation to the entire country."

Still chuckling, Elspeth spread her arms. "I'll hold them back even at risk to my own life," she promised with mock solemnity.

"Um...excuse me?"

Both Perry and Elspeth froze when someone spoke hesitantly from the doorway.

Dropping her arms, Elspeth turned. "Miss Cole," she said in obvious surprise. "How nice to see you again," she added quickly, calling immediately upon her usual impeccable manners.

Perry didn't know whether to groan or laugh when Kristin stepped into his office. Acutely aware of the scattered papers, his wrinkled, stained shirt, his damp hair and the ink on his forehead, he moved toward her. "Hello, Kristin. This is a pleasant surprise."

Her gaze swept the room, and then his appearance, before she lifted her eyes to his. "I wanted to see your workplace," she commented. "It, um, isn't exactly what I'd expected."

Both Perry and Elspeth laughed in response to her dry tone.

"No, I don't imagine it is," Perry replied.

"It's usually much worse than this," Elspeth informed Kristin gravely. "This is a good day. Now, if you'll excuse me, I think I'll go stick my head in the lunchroom refrigerator."

"Tell Marcus I'll meet with him later, will you?" Perry called after her, without looking away from Kristin.

"I'm sure he'll understand." Elspeth was smiling as she closed the door behind her.

Perry couldn't stop staring at Kristin. He was having trouble believing she was standing there in front of him, when it seemed like so very long since he'd seen her. She looked fresh and beautiful in a sleeveless, fitted, waist-length purple top over a matching short straight skirt, and black, chunky-heeled sandals. She'd swept her dark hair up off her neck, probably in deference to the heat, and tasteful diamond studs glinted from her ears. Her brown eyes swept over him again, making him painfully aware of his own uncharacteristically disheveled appearance.

"Bad day?" she asked, a deliberately droll understatement.

"It was—until you showed up," he replied.

Still in a teasing mood, Kristin circled him slowly. "And to think I was worried about being overly influenced by your pretty appearance," she murmured.

He felt heat stain his cheeks, even as he laughed. "Okay, I know I'm a mess. The air conditioner died and my pen exploded."

She stepped directly in front of him. "It doesn't matter," she assured him. "You're still much prettier than any man has a right to be."

He laughed, his day much brighter now that she was in it. "Thank you...I think."

Her smile faded. "I've missed you, Perry."

"I've missed you, too," he answered with a groan. "When I couldn't reach you during the past few days, I thought—"

"I had some serious thinking to do," she interrupted. "I needed time and space to do it in."

Nerves tightened his stomach. "And what were you thinking?"

"I was thinking that I'm still not crazy about politics. While I'll admit the process is more important than I've given it credit for, and that you've convinced me there are some very decent, dedicated politicians among the cons and crooks, I still don't care for the scheming and maneuvering and calculated deliberations involved in even the most well-intentioned campaigns."

He nodded. "I can understand that. And while I will probably always be involved in campaigns that are particularly important to me, I've been giving strong consideration to taking one of the university positions I've been offered. I would be teaching a subject I enjoy, and it would mean much less time on the road."

Kristin nodded consideringly. "I like the sound of that—as long as it's something you really want to do."

"I think it is." He moved toward her, but she held up a hand to hold him off.

"That isn't all I've been thinking about."

He paused. "What else?"

"I'm not an easy person to live with, Perry. No matter how much I would like to be at times, I'm really not spontaneous. I like to make lists. I like to check things off as I accomplish them. I like planning ahead. And then sometimes all my plans come undone when I get distracted with my writing and lose track of time. Sometimes I go for days without surfacing for air. People talk to me and I don't even hear them. It has been known to drive people crazy. Even people who love me."

"But not people who truly understand you," he answered gently, knowing she was referring to former lovers who hadn't. "I've read your books, Kristin. All of them. They're very good. And they didn't get that way without hard work and intense concentration. To try to interfere with that would be to try to change who you are. And why would anyone who loves you want to change you?"

"I have a few problems with trust," she continued. "And with self-confidence."

He nodded again. "I have a few problems of my own. But I can't imagine there's anything the two of us couldn't overcome, if we made an effort. I'm willing to make that effort."

"So am I," she whispered. "I love you, Perry. I want to marry you...if the offer is still open."

"The offer will be open for the rest of my life," he said simply, his heart and his hopes soaring. "I love you more than I've ever loved anyone before. Body and soul, I've belonged to you since you 'bought' me—and I always will."

"No refunds," she whispered, her eyes bright.

"No returns," he added, reaching for her. "I love you, Kristin. Marry me."

"Yes," she said, going into his arms and lifting her face to his. "Yes."

He kissed her until they were both on the verge of passing out from lack of oxygen. And then he kissed her again. He couldn't seem to stop. It astonished him how quickly his day had been transformed from the worst in his life to the most blissfully happy.

A long time later, he drew back reluctantly to look at her. And then he couldn't help laughing.

She lifted an eyebrow. "What's so funny?" she asked, her voice still breathless.

Several strands had escaped from her formerly neatly upswept hair, and now they clung damply to her neck and face. There were smudges of black ink from his hand at the waist and hip of her formerly crisp purple outfit, and another streak of ink on her cheek. Her lipstick had been kissed away—and was probably now decorating his face—and her face was flushed. She looked absolutely beautiful, he thought, falling in love with her all over again.

"Marry me soon," he demanded, impatient for their life together to begin.

She nodded. "I'll try to make short lists," she promised.

He laughed and pulled her to him again, no longer caring whether either of them left this office in reputable condition. "You do that," he murmured, and covered her mouth with his again.

Epilogue

THEY WERE MARRIED in the fall, at the little church
in Cutter's Point where Kristin had been baptized
as a child. The wedding was followed by a small
reception at the nearby country club. The guest list
had been limited to family and close friends, rather
than the mobs of acquaintances they could have invited had they chosen to indulge in a splashy spec-
tacle instead of a quiet, intimate celebration of their
union.

They would be honeymooning in the Caribbean.
Perry couldn't wait to get started. As soon as cour-
tesy allowed, he touched Kristin's arm. "Ready to
go?" he asked, barely reining in his impatience.

She smiled, looking almost as eager as he was.
"Yes. I'm ready."

Sophie bustled up to them, in her element as the
center of attention at her daughter's wedding reception. "Darlings," she said, including them both
in a group hug. "I'm so very happy for you."

She gave each of them a smacking kiss, leaving
blotches of red lipstick on both their cheeks. "Now,
go get started on your honeymoon," she ordered,
smiling brightly at Perry.

"Yes, ma'am," he agreed fervently. He slid an
arm around Kristin's waist and escorted her to the
door, weaving their way through the small crowd
of smiling well-wishers. Kristin's maid of honor

was waiting with Kristin's purse. Kristin thanked her and tucked the leather bag under her arm.

Perry frowned. "Wait a minute," he said.

Poised on the threshold, Kristin looked up in question. "Did you forget something?"

Grinning, he took her purse from beneath her arm, opened it and took out her notebook. And then he turned to Sophie. "Hang on to this for a couple of weeks, will you?" he asked gravely. "When it comes to my honeymoon, there are some things I'd rather not see in a romance novel later."

Sophie laughed delightedly. "My daughter has definitely made the right choice," she said, tucking the notebook safely into her own bag.

Kristin was smiling when Perry turned back to her. "You'll find that I have a very good memory," she warned him.

He looped his arm through hers. "I'll just have to learn to live with it."

Side by side, they walked out the door to begin their own happily-ever-after future.

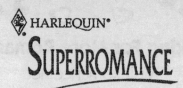

Temptation®

COMING NEXT MONTH

#733 ONE WILD WEEKEND Rita Clay Estrada
Bachelor Auction

Buying time with renowned photographer Archer was
Melody Chase's last chance. She needed to know how to land a
man, and who better qualified to tell her than someone who
spent his life dealing with desirable women? The problem was,
Archer decided he wanted Melody for himself...for only one
wild weekend.

#734 SEXY AS SIN Meg Lacey

When Chastity Goodwin saw sexy Sin O'Connor roar up to her
door on a motorcycle, she knew she was in for a fight. No way
was this man going to willingly replace his black leather and
denim for a doublet and tights—not even for his brother's
wedding! But Sin was full of surprises. And willing to take off
his clothes...as long as Chastity did, too.

#735 WHILE HE WAS SLEEPING Carolyn Andrews
The Wrong Bed

Hopeless romantic Daisy Hanover wasn't looking forward to
her upcoming marriage of convenience. So when she discovered
a quaint country inn, boasting a bed that promised wedded bliss
to the couple who shared it, Daisy made arrangements for her
fiancé to meet her. After one night, Daisy definitely found bliss.
Only, the man in her bed _wasn't_ her fiancé!

#736 BRAZEN Carly Phillips
Blaze

After agreeing to a loveless marriage, Samantha Reed decided
to run away for a week and experience a lifetime's worth of
passion—even if it was with a stranger! Sexy bartender
Ryan "Mac" Mackenzie seemed like the perfect man to love and
leave behind. Only, Mac wasn't a bartender—and he wasn't
letting Samantha go anywhere....